Calamity at KRYME COTTAGE

A BELINDA LAWRENCE MYSTERY

I0638716

BRIAN KAVANAGH

VIVID
PUBLISHING

To discover more Brian Kavanagh books,
or to contact the author, please visit
www.vividpublishing.com.au/briankavanagh

Copyright © 2020 Brian Kavanagh

ISBN: 978-1-922409-67-6
Published by Vivid Publishing
A division of the Fontaine Publishing Group
P.O. Box 948 Fremantle
Western Australia 6959
www.vividpublishing.com.au

To the memory of William & Dorothy Kavanagh without whom this entertainment would not have been written.

For my old and new mates, John Alaimo, Peter Lamb, Clifton Davidson, Gail Hewlett, Pam Barden, Di Morrissey, Bruce McNaughton, Lynn Barker, Ken Sallows, Helen Carmichael, Jean Clark, Murray Fahey, Keith McCarthy, Arthur Kendy, Peter McBain, Tom Jeffrey, Bruce Smeaton, Ross Hamilton, Meredith Whitford, Heather Truskinger, Marsha Holtz, Diana Hockley, Margaret Tanner, Oleg Zolotov, Mare Fairchild, Jeannie & Louis Rigod, Faye Tollison, Bridie & Amelia Jane, Heiko Schneider, Joanne Davidson, and all who's paths have crossed. I can't say it hasn't been fun. (If I've missed you...well, it's way past my bedtime.)

ABOUT THE AUTHOR

Producer/Director/Editor/Writer

With many years experience in film production Brian Kavanagh's career covers the areas of Production, Direction, Editing and Writing on features and documentaries.

Kavanagh is an accredited member of the Australian Screen Editors (A.S.E) by which he was honoured with a Lifetime Achievement Award in 1997 for his contribution to film making in Australia.

He is also a member of the Australian Society of Authors (A.S.A.).

A CRIME

Thud! A body hit the damp earth with a squelch. Two shadowy creatures stood erect: one wheezing, the other wiping hands on dark fabric already taking in muddy fluid. And guilt.

In the Somerset night's pitch black, the only light flowed from a torch resting against a pile of rocks. Its beam played over the scene transfiguring the beings into sinister phantoms as the two reached for shovel and spade. The macabre scene was tempered with the faint perfume of lavender.

The first sod of earth fell into the roughhewn grave. The grave diggers peered into its blackness and could just make out the body twisted to one side, the head at an awkward angle. Soil had fallen on the corpse and was already absorbing the crimson blood.

Birds began to twitter in the nearby trees. The gravediggers worked feverishly to fill in the grave. They had to hurry. Soon, weak daylight would start to reveal the horror. Late Autumn leaves scattered over the monstrous grave would eventually cover the sin.

For the time being.

Chapter One

"They've just finished the garden renovations," said Mona Washington, as she cleared away the breakfast dishes. "I told them they had to have it all finished before you got back from Australia."

Belinda Lawrence drank the last of her coffee. "Thanks, Mona, you did a splendid job while I was away. You always do."

"There's been a few changes recently," continued Mona, "old mister Davidson next door, has gone to live with his sister, Bev, over in Wells. There's a young man in there now, an artist or writer or something frivolous like that. Unmarried. There's a new Vicar over at St Mathew's in Abbey Combe. 'Not married, a typical Vicar, or so I'm told by Miss Atkins, and that malicious gossip Muriel Meldrew - you remember them? They do the flowers and brass, so I suppose they know what they're talking about. 'Likely the old dozy sort who sings off-key at Evensong, and wears odd socks."

She nodded her head in the staircase's general direction, which set off an explosion of creaks and cracks from her neck. "A letter arrived from the vicarage. It's on the stand near the stairs. From him, no doubt. Probably planning to drop in for a free afternoon tea. Make sure he doesn't make a habit of it." She paused as she mentally ran through the list of things that happened while Belinda was away from Milford. "Oh, and at last, Kryme Cottage has been sold," she added, as she wiped her hands on a faded Wills & Kate Wedding tea towel.

"Really?" said Belinda as she rose from the kitchen table, "it's been empty now for, how long?"

"About as long as I've been working for you. Five or six years," said Mona with mock indifference.

Belinda sensed discontentment behind this reply. "Well, thanks again for doing a good job of getting the garden repaired. I want it to be looking its best by May when the summer tourists begin to arrive."

Mona was tying on an apron. "You've made quite a success of it, haven't you, Miss, since your Aunt left you this cottage, and you discovered the secret about who designed the garden. All those wealthy garden fanatics traipsing about. 'Made quite a penny out of it, I'm sure." Her last comment had a touch of tartness.

Belinda smiled to herself. Mona was always hinting that her housekeeping services where undervalued, but she believed that the remuneration Mona received was more than satisfactory when she was required to supervise the garden tours whenever Belinda was away. "Yes," said Belinda, "garden lovers certainly are keen to see one of the rare, small gardens that Capability Brown designed."

Mona raised an eyebrow. "He usually did landscapes, didn't he? I remember you telling me... famous for them. Apparently. Mmm." Mona appeared to be lost in thought for a moment, before snapping, "I've been meaning to tell you, Miss. I don't think I can continue doing it now, after all, I'm not getting any younger." As if to illustrate this claim, she touched at her greying hair, gently patting it into place, although to Belinda's eye, it was so tightly constrained by a tangerine crocheted hair net it would need a hurricane to dislodge even one strand. "And my daughter is keen for me to move closer to her in Bristol, so I'm considering that."

Belinda studied the older woman. Not more than fifty-five was her assessment, along with the belief that Mona was living up to her name and was not so very subtly indicating that she would consider continuing in her role for extra compensation. "Thank you for letting me know, Mona, I'll be sorry to lose you, but you must do what is best for you. I'll start looking for someone to replace you, which will be difficult, I'm sure." Mona Washington gave a weedy smile. It wasn't going to plan.

Belinda, recovered now from a long flight from Australia (a good ten-hour sleep had undeniable restorative powers), walked to the entrance hall and took an envelope from the stand. Opening it, she read, *'Allow me to introduce myself. I'm Charles Mead, and I write to you as I know you were a good friend of Reverend Lawson, who was so cruelly murdered here some years ago. As I have been appointed vicar at St Mathew's, I would like to meet with you when you return from Australia. Please call on me at any time.'*

Why underline it, thought Belinda, and why did he seem so keen to meet? Did he have something important to tell her? She glanced down at the handwritten note. The writing was formal, strong, and masculine,

Mounting the stairs, Belinda felt a moment of dread as she recalled the day she discovered her Great Aunt Jane's broken body lying at the foot of the staircase. Her inheritance in Milford's tiny village on the outskirts of Bath in Somerset, this ancient Bath Stone cottage - nowadays faded gold by the passing of centuries - plus its internationally famous garden had secured her residency in England. However, she still held allegiance to her hometown of Melbourne in far off Australia.

Walking to a spare bedroom, she checked that Mona had prepared everything in readiness for the arrival of her friend, Hazel Whitby. Satisfied that all was in order, she walked to the window and looked down on the next-door property. While old Mr. Davidson had lived there, his whole garden, which reached down to the edge of Belinda's cottage, had been given over to growing vegetables, and often she had been the recipient of gifted cauliflowers, Brussel sprouts, and, in the summer, gorgeous fresh tomatoes. That had started how many years ago?

With her recent birthday just passed, Belinda had decided to admit to no longer being in her late twenties; besides, her age was her business, and the thirties promised to be as adventurous as previous decades. All the former vegetarian cornucopia was now gone, and Belinda could see the new resident was converting the space into a well-designed cottage garden. She wondered what the newcomer to the village was like. Artist or writer, Mona had suggested. Either way, the man sounded interesting, and Belinda felt she should meet him. It would be the neighbourly thing to do. She smiled to herself.

The weak sun broke through the morning mists, and it seemed set for a wonderful late Autumn day. A visit to the new Vicar at St Mathew's might provide a pleasant walk; he did say, 'please call on me at any time.'

Changing into woollen trousers, a Cherry red high neck polo top, and comfortable sneakers, she brushed her auburn hair, topped it with a black French beret, applied some lipstick, slipped into a warm woollen coat, and taking a duty-free bottle of Australian Shiraz as a gift – if he didn't drink he could use it at the Lord's Supper – she set off on her way. By the gate, she glanced around at her newly repaired garden. It would take some time to walk through it all, as it spread way down the hill to the local Pub, the general meeting place for the village's few inhabitants. With her cottage, the total was no more than ten residences.

Bending down, she gathered a few remaining Mei-kyo Chrysanthemums, their pompom flowers would be ideal for placing on her Aunt Jane's grave, which was in the churchyard at Abbey Combe.

Out in the street, she walked up the few yards to the corner and old Mr. Davidson's cottage. It crossed her mind to call and introduce herself to the new neighbour, but the place was silent and had the air of waiting. Waiting for its new owner to return home and breathe new life into it. Probably best, Belinda thought. Meeting two new neighbours in one day might prove to be exhausting, and she set off along the path leading to Abbey Combe.

A thought occurred that she should have telephoned the Reverend to see if he was at the vicarage, and she felt for her mobile phone only to realise she had left it on the dresser in her bedroom. It might prove to be a wasted journey. Still, the fresh country air was invigorating and cleared away all the angst associated with international jet travel, which even flying first class could never wholly eradicate, so she continued happily on her way.

The path began to dip down into a hollow shrouded by many Holm Oaks, crowded together with Holly and Sweet Chestnuts. Combined, their weighty foliage blocked out the sun, transforming the sweet country air into a damp and musty glen. Belinda shivered in the sudden transition from the sun's cheery warmth to a chill, dark and melancholy landscape.

Silence held sway.

A ground cover accumulation of hedging plants, self-seeded from nearby mother hedges, fought for control over various plants; sweet cicely, wood sage, stinging nettle, bound together by numerous creepers, crowding the pathway and reducing it to a narrow track.

Within this dark passage, a dilapidated 'FOR SALE 'Abernathy and Ffrench signboard rested at a crazy angle, the freshly posted 'SOLD' in bright red lettering splashed across the weathered panel proclaiming that Kryme Cottage was to be revived and present a new face to the world.

Belinda had passed by the Cottage many times but had never paid it much attention. It had always been half-hidden by trees and shrubs, and she'd always thought it must be dank and unhealthy. She recalled years back, when she had first moved to Milford, the local villagers had hinted that Kryme was haunted, but none could agree on the reason; some claimed a murder had taken place there back in the late eighteenth century; others that a woman and her disfigured daughter had lived there in Victorian times and were witches. They'd held séances and called up the devil before disappearing one stormy night and then vanished off the earth's face.

Others told of a mysterious woman in black who always arrived by carriage at night, was never seen by the villagers. She stayed for only a few days and departed again by moonlight, her horse and carriage rumbling through the silent night, disturbing the villagers sleep and dreams, causing sleepy mutterings of prayer that sought protection from the nocturnal riot.

Curiosity got the better of Belinda, and stepping cautiously through the mixture of vines and creepers that threatened to snare her feet, she pushed open the half-rotten wooden gate and edged her way towards the door of the cottage.

The Limestone had long surrendered its

pale glow to a cover of lichen and dust of the ages. Belinda estimated the original building to be older than some village houses, but Kryme had been renovated sometime in the nineteenth century and presented a then-fashionable Georgian facade.

The solid wooden door was central with a shuttered window on either side. Some of the wooden slats were broken, affording Belinda an opportunity to peer into one of the front rooms. A wasted expectation, as the exterior gloom had penetrated the building and all was dark and secretive. A faint click nearby made Belinda turn and she saw the door, very slowly, edge open.

Just a fraction.

Startled, Belinda moved to the door. It had opened just enough to reveal a glimpse of a rough stone wall. Was someone in the house? All was silent. "Hello? Is anyone there?" Again silence. Belinda glanced back at the footpath. The shadowy trees undulated in a soft breeze. She gave a shiver recalling the story that the house was haunted. Nonsense, she told herself, turned back to the door and gave it a gentle push. To her surprise, it gave way quickly and swung silently open. She called again, but there was no reply. Cautiously she stepped over the threshold into a short entrance hall.

Chapter Two

It was apparent to Belinda the building's age was much like her own cottage, which had its origins in the 13th century; indeed, Kryme was probably much older. The walls and floor were solid stone, and as she progressed inwards through the gloom, she saw the building was essentially one large chamber. The light from the open door revealed a small room on either side, which appeared to be wooden divisions constructed later. Dead leaves collected on the uneven stone floor while here and there, dull cobwebs hung like morbid ornamentations.

Turning left, she entered what would appear to have been a living room. A large smoke-stained fireplace dominated the space. A broken chair and worn sofa were the only remnants of the previous habitation. The other room was empty, and Belinda made her way further into the cottage.

The main structure was a large space and much more extensive than she'd imagined, longer and stretching back into the surrounding trees. Little light seeping into the area came from a few narrow upright windows set well back in the thick stone walls. Here and there, small hollows in the walls were presumably designed to contain candles.

A slight scuffling sound and Belinda was face to face with a tiny mouse scampering onto a windowsill. It paused to view this intruder, shiny black eyes assessing the situation, before pleasingly dropping from sight.

Moving on, the remainder of the expanse was bare; the warped undulating stone floor showed signs of disturbance, and once or twice, Belinda caught her foot on a raised fragment and stumbled. Cautiously she continued until she reached the rear wall, which was shaped in a half-circle. Nearby was a small compact staircase, and again, this appeared to be a later addition. The wooden steps showed signs of repair over time and creaked ominously as she ascended, to reach two small empty rooms sitting on the roof of the building, each with a pocket-sized window and a sloping skylight also from a later period. In one, a wooden miniature cupboard had been built into the corner. Belinda tried to open the door, but it was firmly locked. The latch was a strange design of a devil's face, hooked nose, squinting eyes, and a gaping mouth waiting to devour the key.

The reverberation of the front door slamming made Belinda jump in fright, and she held her breath as heavy footsteps made their way through the cottage. Thinking it best to reveal her presence, she began to descend the stairs. "Hello, I'm sorry to intrude," she called, "I was passing and liked the cottage so much, I just had to..." She stopped at the foot of the stairs.

There was no reply.

Silence.

The cottage was empty.

A shadow of panic overcame her, and she hurried along the rough stone floor to the entrance.

Grasping the door handle, it would not turn. She fought to free it from the lock. The rattle of the door mocked her. Far back behind, she heard the footsteps returning. Desperate now, she increased pressure on the handle. It seemed to be physically challenging her. The footsteps were louder. Belinda glanced over her shoulder. The dark space appeared to be empty.

With one final effort, she wrenched the handle, and it miraculously freed itself from the lock, allowing the door to swing easily on its hinges, revealing sanctuary and freedom. Belinda rushed to the path, stumbling over the mosaic of vines and creepers. She paused, took a deep breath, and turned to look at the cottage. The open door, mocking her, began to close slowly, and a soft click once again sealed the cottage from the outside world.

***

The Reverend Charles Mead was a tall solid man with handsome, rugged features; a sportsman's frame filled his black clerical shirt, quite unlike any of the previous Vicars at St Mathew's. His hair was cut short and close to his head, while brown eyes looked judgmentally from behind fashionable tortoiseshell frames. The hair was dark, but here and there, little slivers of silver flashed. Belinda estimated he was about forty. "I thought we should meet as we have something that connects us," he said, as he poured the Australian wine into two glasses. With a smile, he handed one to Belinda, who accepted it while giving him a questioning look.

"Really? In what way are we connected?"

Reverend Mead raised his glass as though in a toast. "Murder." He took an appreciative sip of wine, considered it for a time, and nodded. "Hmmm...deep black fruit. Intense high grade oak. A joy... extraordinary."

Belinda choked back a laugh. "Reverend, you mean it doesn't taste of chocolate, vanilla, the scent of roses grown on the shores of the Mediterranean, or your grandmother's treacle tart?"

The Reverend lowered his glass, having taken another draught of the excellent wine. "I think, seeing we are near neighbours and you are cynical about my judgement of wine, a cynicism I intend to overcome, calling me reverend will become tiresome. Call me, Charles."

Belinda smiled. "Of course...Charles. And you must call me Belinda."

"I'm led to believe it was you who found your murdered aunt in her cottage," said Charles as he took a seat nearby, "and those stalwarts of scandalmongering, Misses Atkins and Meldrew, assure me it was you who also discovered the reverend Lawson when he was mutilated and murdered here in this very room?"

Belinda placed her wine glass on a side table. "Put that way, you make it sound as though I make a habit of it."

"But don't you? Apart from those two murders, I hear you're also an amateur sleuth, which would, I assume, place you close to crime and the occasional homicide."

Belinda gave him an appraising glance. "You seem rather preoccupied with murder."

"Sin." Charles gave a wide smile. "I'm preoccupied with sin, and since murder was the first sin committed –"

"I thought disobedience was an earlier sin. The apple and all that," said Belinda as she reached for her glass and took a sip.

Charles looked thoughtful. "Hmmm...academic. But being slaughtered with the jawbone of an ass by your brother, I think, takes precedence. Venial versus mortal."

"Did he really use a jawbone?"

Charles shrugged. "Maybe. Maybe not. But murdered, Abel was, and that is a sin."

Belinda began to feel they were drifting into ecclesiastical waters. She ran her eye over his solid frame, and Mona's words came back to her, 'the dozy sort who sings off-key at Evensong, and wears odd socks.' She shifted in her seat and glanced down at his ankles; his matching socks were scarlet.

Charles caught her glance and self-consciously moved his feet to allow the hem of his trousers to fall like a veil, removing the scarlet surprise from sight. It was almost a demure action, as though the colourful leggings hinted at some frivolity best kept hidden from the world. He challenged Belinda's look when she lifted her eyes. "Charles, forgive me for asking, but I'm a little confused. I'd been led to believe that you – or the new vicar – was, how should I put it, well a much older man."

Charles gave a mild snort of amusement. "Now who's been telling you that?"

"My housekeeper, Mona. It seems that some gossip had –"

"Stop." Charles raised his hand. "It can only have been Misses Atkins and Muriel Meldrew, my diligent and gossip mongering helpers. But they would have been talking about the reverend Lamb."

"Lamb?"

"Hmmm...more or less set for retirement when this gig came up. Caught the London train from Durham and was never seen again."

"What? But Misses Whatevertheirnames suggested to Mona, the Vicar was dull and probably wore odd socks, which I imagine would indicate that they thought it typical. So, never arrived here? How would they know what the Vicar was like?"

"That description would just about fit any Vicar."

Belinda was thoughtful. "Maybe jumped off the train? Was a body ever found?"

Charles shook his head. "No. No one remembers."

"Maybe never got on the train?"

"A suitcase was found when the train got to Kings Cross. There were one or two supposed sightings. One in Chelsea and one in Wells, but they came to nothing. Was listed as a missing person, and I was appointed vicar here."

Belinda linked her fingers together. "Wells is not far from Bath, might have been confused, and got lost somewhere in Somerset?"

"Well, the reverend is still lost. The police have put it in the too hard basket. Plenty of old men and women go off and are never seen again."

Belinda felt Charles was being a little un-Christian. She looked at him as he reclined in his comfortable chair. "Well, I suppose it was an ill wind that did blow some good. You got the gig, as you say. You've made little change to the vicarage from the reverend Lawson's day. Have you got to know the parishioners at all?"

Charles put his empty glass down, relaxed, stretched out his legs, and placed his hands behind his head. "I'm making inroads. There has been some resistance to a newcomer, but I think I'm winning them over. 'Even had a visit from another newcomer to the village, Madam Malefic. Another potential brass polisher and flower arranger."

Belinda frowned. Mona hadn't mentioned this woman's name, and that was unusual as she prided herself on knowing all the comings and goings in Milford.

"Madam Malefic?" said Belinda, "where is she living?"

Charles sensed her feminine curiosity and grinned. "Nowhere at the moment, but she's about to take up residency in Kryme Cottage."

Chapter Three

Belinda gasped in surprise. "Kryme Cottage? Why I've just been there." She explained her experience to Charles, who listened intently. "They say it's haunted, and after what I experienced, I can believe it," she concluded.

"You believe in ghosts?" said Charles casually.

Belinda sensed he was teasing her. "Well, I've known a few odd things that can't be explained," she said and drank the last of her wine.

"Odd things? Can you elaborate?"

Belinda wasn't prepared to play his game. She toyed with her empty glass. "I'd rather not, besides, I don't think you'd believe me."

Charles gave a grin and was about to reply, but Belinda cut him off. "And as for Kryme cottage, the locals believe it's haunted, and apparently there was a murder there some time -"

" And we're back to murder," interrupted Charles.

They both were silent for a moment as they exchanged a glance.

***

As Belinda retraced her steps home, she reflected on Charles' comments. The two murders she'd witnessed in Milford, her Great Aunt Jane's and the Reverend Lawson's, had indeed led her to be something of a sleuth. The first crime exposed fanatics prepared to kill to secure ownership of her Aunt's small garden designed by Capability Brown and of value because of its rarity. The second, a pseudo-religious group fixated with a scrap of ancient tapestry she had discovered, which the leader sought to validate his claim to the English throne. This tapestry led to Reverend Lawson's gruesome murder while strengthening her friendship with Hazel Whitby and their subsequent partnership in the world of antiques. This ecosphere revealed a hotbed of criminals prepared to murder to gain possession of rare and historical objects.

These thoughts occupied her as she walked, and it was with some surprise that she found herself once more outside Kryme Cottage. A cheerful whistle alerted her to the presence of a young man climbing a ladder to replace some broken roof tiles. He glanced at her and gave a cheery smile before whistling on his way to the roof. Beyond the open door, she could see tradesmen painting the walls. The footsteps she'd heard? Could they have been the workers beginning repair? Belinda was doubtful. The FOR SALE sign had been removed. The cottage was being prepared for the arrival of Madam Malefic.

***

Hazel Whitby turned the key to Belinda's cottage door and, hauling a large suitcase, made her way upstairs to the spare bedroom. The journey had been an exhausting one, from her small Antique shop on Pulteny Bridge, to her apartment in Lansdown Crescent, for eagle-eyed supervision of the extensive restoration work being undertaken there. She collapsed on the bed to regain her strength. The days of ample energy were in the past, and Hazel had to admit, if only to herself, that the years were ticking by and growing old gracefully was her only option. Turning fifty had been a milestone, but that was some years ago, and she was not looking forward to yet another benchmark.

The cottage was silent, and it was clear Mona Washington had finished her work for the day, but where was Belinda? She fumbled for her mobile phone and tapped Belinda's stored number, but was surprised when the phone rang near in Belinda's bedroom. She rose and looked. The phone was on the dresser. Odd that Belinda should go out without taking her phone.   Moving back to her room, she began the task of unpacking her suitcase. Glancing out the window, she saw a man digging in the next-door garden. Presumably, it was hard work as he stopped to wipe his brow, and she watched with interest as he pulled off his heavy crewneck jumper leaving him in only a T-shirt and jeans.

Tight jeans.

Hazel reached for her mobile phone. She'd

heard that old Mr Davidson had moved, so this was the new resident? She raised the phone and took a series of photographs as the man continued to dig. The hole was getting to be quite deep when he stopped, laid down the spade, and tipped a sizeable hessian bag into the hole, the contents of which Hazel could only guess at. Wiping his brow again, he began to shovel earth over the bag until it was fully buried.

Hazel watched with interest as his muscular arms completed the task. In a Pavlovian reaction, she automatically reached for the perfume she'd bought recently in Paris, *J'ai de la chance*, and put a dab behind each ear.

Patting the earth flat with the spade, the man stood erect, took a deep breath, and reached for his jumper. As he put it on, he glanced up at Belinda's overlooking wall and directly at the window where Hazel was standing. Hazel did not attempt to move or conceal the fact she was watching him. He stared at her for a moment, then turned and walked back across the garden to enter his cottage.

Hazel gave a satisfied smile and began to hang clothes in the cupboard. A new man in her life? What she had seen was pleasing and augured well for the time she would be staying with Belinda over the coming Christmas period.

***

Quentin de La Tour dropped the spade into its customary place, turned, and began to wash his hands at the laundry sink. From there, he watched as the female figure moved back and forth at the window of the adjoining cottage. From what he could see of the woman, she appeared to be a well preserved fifty. Fifty-five? Dark hair. Attractive. But he was confused. He'd been led to believe by Mona, the woman who gave the impression she was the cottage's housekeeper, the owner was a younger woman. Thirty, or so. He grinned. A mystery to be solved.

Since moving to Milford from London, he'd found village life to be not as relaxing as he'd anticipated. Getting to know the locals and being accepted by them had been more challenging than he'd thought. Still, he was making some headway by joining them on nights at the Ship & Anchor pub for a pint of Bath beer or an extra cunning Scrumpy, both of which seemed to make the residents more affable. Especially when he was buying. This was often followed by an evening meal of steak with garlic sauce, and their famous Chunky Fries producing a lovely crunchy outside and a deliciously fluffy, creamy middle. Gorged, he would negotiate the dark path up the hill to his new home and reflect on the small pleasures that life can offer.

At the pub one stormy night, in answer to his queries about the history of the village, some slightly squiffy responses entertained him with tales of headless horsemen, various ghosts and ghoulies. Claims by the assembled drinkers, with unified nods of heads and mutterings, were made of murder, witches, séances, a tormented young girl, turbulent nights, manifestations. One drinker had a most intriguing anecdote of a shadowy woman in black, who arrived at night by horse and carriage. After a few days during which she was never seen in the village, she left again, always by moonlight, the terror her carriage wheels and horses hooves reverberating through the night. It was thus that Quentin learned of Kryme Cottage.

Chapter Four

Some weeks had passed, and now, with the beginning of December, Belinda searched through old recipe books that had belonged to her Aunt Jane. Her parents were due to arrive from Melbourne in a day or so to spend Christmas in Bath, and being a dutiful daughter, Belinda was planning a sumptuous dinner for the twenty-fifth, as it was a rare chance for them to be together.

"Which hotel are they staying at?" said Hazel, sifting through cocktail recipes.

"Chestnut, bacon & parsnip soup," pondered Belinda, as she turned a page. "Hmm? Hotel? At The New Abbey. Dad says it will be too cold here at the cottage, so he wants central heating, and Mum wanted something near Sally Lunn's as she'll be gorging herself on the buns there. But they will come here for meals, and we can join them for afternoon tea. Do you think braised red cabbage with cider & apples would go well at Christmas dinner?"

"How many will there be?" said Hazel, as she tried to decide between Amaretto fizz and Raspberry Champagne cocktail.

"With Mum and Dad and us, four. And I'll ask the vicar."

Hazel's eyebrows shot up. "Really?"

Belinda turned back to the recipe book to avoid Hazel's enquiring eyes. "Why not? He's new in the parish, and it seems a neighbourly thing to do. He may not come of course."

"I see," said Hazel dryly. "Well, if you're having a boyfriend, I want our next door neighbour."

Belinda looked at her. "We don't even know him. Besides, he doesn't seem to have been in the cottage for weeks."

"Yes, he has. I've seen him."

"He may not be available."

"Oh, I think he's available," said Hazel, smouldering.

Once again, Belinda realised her friend was about to make another conquest. "As you say, it would be a neighbourly thing to do," added Hazel with an annoying smirk.

Realising she had no choice, Belinda reached for a note pad and began to write. "As mister Davidson's moved and the phone may have been switched off, I'll drop a note asking him to afternoon tea tomorrow, so we can meet him and see what he's like."

Belinda made her way to the neighbouring cottage. The weather was threatening. A glance at the thundery clouds meant she should hurry and drop the invitation in his letterbox and return home before the storm broke, putting to flight what little light there was. Hazel's implied suggestion that the Vicar was her 'boyfriend' irked her, although she did find him attractive, to be honest. Could she be a Vicar's wife? She snorted and admonished herself for having such a ridiculous thought. But hidden away, the idea took refuge in the Limbic system in her brain, there to await resuscitation.

She turned the corner and just reached the cottage door when she was distracted by a strange noise. It took her a moment to realise what it was.

The sound of horses galloping.

The crunch of wheels on a hard surface.

She turned to see a hair-raising apparition hurtling down the Bath Road and turning wildly into the path to Abbey Combe. The sinister carriage approached rapidly and threatened to run her down.

Just in time, she leaned back against the cottage door. The horses, nostrils flaring, eyes wild and menacing, snorted as they thundered closer. Following, she saw what appeared to be a large menacing Victorian baby carriage, with two small wheels at the front, two large wheels at the back. A dark leather hood was unfolded, covering the driver and one passenger.

Belinda caught a glimpse of a woman in black, her stark white face in contrast to the gloom. The carriage passed within inches of her, horses hooves pounding the earth, wheels spinning towards her.

Frightened, she pressed further back into the door, which unexpectedly gave way and she fell back, only to be caught up in strong arms. "What's all this racket?" said Quentin, as he held Belinda upright. He leaned forward over her shoulder to see the disappearing carriage. "Hmm, an old Phaeton." He turned back to Belinda. "Are you alright?"

But the pale features on this strange female

shivering now in his arms indicated all was not well. "No, I can see you aren't." Lifting Belinda up, he moved into the cottage, sat her down on a sofa, wrapped a woollen rug around her, and reached for a decanter. "A drop of brandy is called for, I think."

Belinda forced herself to take deep breaths as the dizziness and shock she had suffered started to ease. She began to take in her surroundings, and slowly her mind cleared to remember she had been on her way to visit her neighbour, and now it seems he was standing before her offering a glass of brandy.

"Sip this and try and relax," said Quentin. Belinda reached for the glass and took a gulp, letting the fiery liquid course down, spreading its warmth. Her heartbeat began to return to normal. Over the rim of the glass, she looked at her rescuer. He smiled down at her. "I'm Quentin. May I ask who you are?"

Belinda imagined Hazel's description of him; a 'hunk', was the pigeon-hole in which she would have placed him. She smiled as she recalled her mother's snide observation of Hazel's love life, 'all those countless male organisms that inhabit her estrogenic nesting box.'
Belinda swallowed another sip of brandy. "I'm your neighbour, Belinda Lawrence."

Quentin frowned. This stranger was nothing like the woman he'd seen in the window of the neighbouring cottage. "I've been away this week and haven't had a chance to introduce myself, but I thought an older woman was living next door?"

Belinda grinned. "Oh, that would be Hazel Whitby, my business partner. She's staying with me at the moment."

"Business? What..."

"Antiques. Mainly silver and bric-a-brac here in Bath, and in Wells, we deal with period furniture." She drank the last of the brandy, placed the glass on a side table, and rose from the sofa. Quentin put out his hand to steady her. "No, I'm alright now, thanks. I came to deliver a note asking you to come to afternoon tea tomorrow, but now I think perhaps drinks would be better. Hazel is practicing making cocktails for Christmas day, so I'm sure she'd appreciate the chance to experiment."

Quentin grinned. "I'm already looking forward to it." He led the way to the door. "What time?"

"About five?" Belinda stepped out into the dark and glanced around. In the distance, a flash of lightning preceded a roll of thunder. There was no sign or sound of the weird and surreal carriage.

"I'll walk you home," said Quentin.

"No, I'll be alright," said Belinda turning to him, "it's only a few yards. Tell me. When that carriage almost ran me down, you called it something. A phantom or something like that."

"It was an old Phaeton."

"And that is...?"

"An open carriage. Rather sporty. With huge wheels and horse drawn. Strange to see one these days."

"Why is that?"

Quentin stroked his chin thoughtfully. "Well, from what I've read, they were popular in the late eighteenth and early nineteenth century."

***

The Vicar waited in the shadows of the oaks and chestnuts. His black liturgical cassock was the complete camouflage, blending into the darkness. As the storm drew closer, Charles watched the restless horses paw the ground, eager to be back in their barn and settled down. Unexpectedly, the distant shadowy figure of a female, joined by a towering hulking male figure, left Kryme Cottage. They clambered into the waiting carriage, the man into the driver's seat. The woman sank back into the dark interior. A twitch of the reins and they thundered past him in the direction of Abby Combe.

Two workmen locked the door behind them and set off for Milford, each trying to outdo each other on the number of pints they would consume at the Ship & Anchor.

Waiting until they were out of sight, Charles slipped from his hiding place, crossed the garden to the cottage porch. Fumbling in his pocket, he produced a key and eased the lock open. The intermittent flashes of lightning augmented the light from his torch. Workmen's tools still filled the rooms, and the smell of fresh paint confirmed the idea there was a new life coming to the old building.

Rolled up rugs indicated the stone floor was to be covered, and it was the floor itself that the Vicar's torchlight searched. The ancient stones were uneven, but what he sought was an indication of a disturbance to the surface made eons ago. Midway into the large room, he dropped to his knees and ran a finger along a small gap separating two of the larger stones.

Chapter Five

"Gin, lemon juice, Maidenii La Tonique, sugar syrup, absinthe," said Hazel, as she placed the lid on the cocktail shaker and dexterously blended the contents with ice. Straining the cocktail into a glass, adding a twist of lemon, she handed it to Quentin. "There, a perfect Walking Dead."

Quentin received the drink with some misgiving. Hazel served another glass to Belinda, who eyed it suspiciously. "If you're planning to serve cocktails on Christmas Day, I suggest you find one with a less alarming name."

Hazel took a judgemental sip from her glass. "You may be right. Not really seasonal, is it? And," she took her place beside Quentin on the sofa, "I suspect we'd all end up as zombies."

They were on the lower-ground floor of Belinda's cottage in the long sitting room, which ran the building's length and where Great Aunt Jane had entertained Belinda on the only occasion they'd met. Nearby was a bathroom and kitchen and the narrow stairs leading up to the bedrooms. The shutters were closed against the late afternoon chill, and the fireplace glowed with warmth and cheer. The room had become a sanctuary filled with benevolence as they sipped their Walking Deads.

Hazel, confident that her direct from Paris perfume *J'ai de la chance* declared her availability, moved a little on the sofa, closer to Quentin. A little too close, as her quarry, discreetly at first and then speedily, edged away. He began to sneeze violently and reached for a handkerchief to cover his nose. Still sneezing, he rose, spilt his cocktail, and staggered across the room to sink down next to Belinda, where she sat by the fire.

Hazel, bewildered by his actions, hurriedly left the room. Quentin continued sneezing until the spasm left him. Sniffing and blowing his nose, he turned to Belinda. "Sorry about that," he said in a thick voice, "it's just that I'm allergic to some things, like overpowering perfumes."

Belinda rose and crossed over to refill his cocktail glass. "Here, this will kill any toxicities, I'm sure," she said with a smile. He took the glass and had a good slug of the exotic mixture. Belinda stood watching him. A curious man, she thought. What was it Mona Washington told her he did? A writer? A painter? She sat beside him again and put some wood on the fire. "What do you do? What work? Or are you a gentleman of leisure?"

Quentin gave a final sneeze. "No such luck, I'm afraid. Photography. Mainly landscape and wildlife. I'm getting interested in doing aerial work. Occasionally, when the bank is broke, it's the dreaded wedding album. But what about you? I've heard various stories of how you came to own this cottage, all including murder."

Belinda sighed and told how her great aunt had been murdered and how a famous landscape designer created the cottage garden. She looked

Quentin in the eye. "As a matter of fact, before old mister Davidson, a murderer lived in your cottage. Jacob. He murdered his sister. And he tried to murder me."

Quentin raised an eyebrow. "Why would anyone want to do that? He must have been mad, to want to do away with someone so lovely."

Belinda dropped her eyes, a small smile playing on her lips. "Now you're being generous." To herself, she thought; he's handsome, pleasant, but something didn't seem right. Leaning back in her chair, she looked at him again. "That horse and carriage last night. You said they were popular in the eighteenth and nineteenth centuries. Why would there be one hurtling through the streets now?"

"I wondered about that, too," said Quentin, "it made me think of a story I heard at the pub one night, about a woman in black, who, many years ago, arrived by horse and carriage, always at night. No one ever saw her in the village, and it was always in the dark when she left."

Belinda snorted. "You heard that at the pub? Rubbish. Just one of the old folk stories they tell when they've had too much Scrumpy."

Quentin stood and placed his cocktail glass on a table. "Possibly. But they tell the secretive woman in black, resided at Kryme Cottage."

Belinda looked startled. "And...and last night, the carriage was heading in that direction."

***

Tea and Sally Lunns made the perfect ending to the day for Mr and Mrs Lawrence, and Belinda walked them back to their nearby hotel. They wanted an early night after they arrived from London, and Mr Lawrence was hoping that tomorrow would see them on their way to Bristol for an inspection of Isambard Kingdom Brunel's mighty ship the S.S. Great Britain. His wife was not that keen on the trip. Still, she had agreed to accompany him after he reluctantly settled to go with her on a three-day tour of Glastonbury's pre-Christian history covering the Celt's belief that Glassy Island, as it was known then, was where the King of the Fairies by name, Gwyn, welcomed the souls of the dead. Mr Lawrence claimed he could just about cope with fairies, but would damned well not be expected to climb Glastonbury Tor.

The dreary grey day was threatening snow, and once Belinda had seen her parents settled in for the night, she drove back home to Milford, eager for the warmth of a stoked fire and maybe some steaming hot chocolate. Snowflakes began to fall as she closed her front door, hung her heavy coat and scarf on the stand, kicked off her shoes, and pushed her feet into the fur-lined Ugg boots she was addicted to when the weather was at its worst. As she did this, she could hear Hazel's voice issuing from the kitchen where she had promised to make the evening meal. Hazel, not known for her culinary skills, relied on a cookbook written by Escoffier and was surprised to read the recipe did not call for more than one glass of red wine. Given her total belief in the life-giving qualities of aroused grape juice, she added three cups of the restorative while periodically sampling it to ensure she was correct in her assessment as to its quality.

Belinda approached the kitchen door when she was halted in her tracks by a sharp tap, tap, tap on the front door. Surprised and wondering who would be calling now as night was setting in, she turned, retraced her steps, and opened the door.

In the darkness, an even gloomier form was manifest. Only the white fringe of snow on hooded head and shoulders separated it from the garden's dark. Belinda switched on the porch light, and the illuminated spectre did little to calm her nerves.

The spectre spoke. "Good evening. I'm Madam Malefic." A bony hand emerged from the black folds of a cloak and thrust a calling card towards Belinda. At the same time, her hood fell back, revealing the gaunt features of a woman of about sixty, with extremely high cheekbones, a determined and pointed jaw, lips unadorned and thin to the point of being superfluous. Only the nose rescued the features from being the prototype for the Wicked Witch of the West; it reposed artfully as if misplaced by Julie Andrews. Gray hair pinned up in a jumble of loose curls sat above coal-black pupils, resolute behind hooded eyelids. Beneath the cloak, a full-length black dress stole a look, while determined button-up boots supported all of the above.

Belinda took a step back in surprise. This encouraged Madam Malefic to stride forward. The movement confused Belinda as it seemed to her the woman had peeled away from the darkness, leaving an image behind her. Then Belinda realised a man had been standing behind the visitor. He also was dressed in black and was of medium height, young, about eighteen, lank brown hair, and standing in a slightly cowered posture. The strong whiff of peppermint hung in the air.

Their visitor continued into the hall regardless of the snow shower dripping from her cloak. "I've newly arrived in Milford," she proclaimed in a surprisingly deep voice, "and introducing myself to the inhabitants. I have purchased Kryme Cottage, where I invite all interested parties to attend my séances, whereby they may speak with their dear departed souls." Belinda glance down at the calling card.

Madam Malefic.
Spiritualist
(Your mediator to the Afterlife)
Drama Coach

Madam Malefic studied Belinda. "You are, I believe, Miss Lawrence? I hear tell that your Great Aunt was foully murdered in this very cottage." Breathing deeply, she glanced towards the ceiling and nodded.

"Yes. Yes, I feel her spirit nearby. Restless. She has much to tell..."

"Talking of telling," said Belinda archly, "would you please tell me what gives you the right to burst in like this? Would you please leave now?"

Madam Malefic studied her. "Ah. A doubting Thomas. But the time will come when you need me."

Hazel, who had been listening at the kitchen door, stepped into the hall. Madam drew herself up to full height and ran a questioning eye over her. "And you would be...?"

"About to serve Daube a la Provençale, and I'd be pleased if you'd take your out-of-body and just bugger off," said Hazel in a voice that, if spoken on stage, would reach the uppermost balcony.

Their unwelcome visitor gave a nod of approval. "Yes. Magnificent. I can use you." She turned and strode out the door calling over her shoulder, "Come, Darcy." The silent young man glanced at Belinda before turning and following the dark woman into the even darker night.

Still stunned by this unexpected apparition, Hazel's beef stew was consumed in total silence. Belinda was amazed at the excellence of the dish as, up until now, Hazel's cooking skills consisted of cups of tea and the occasional boiled egg. Hunger pains now placated, Belinda reflected on the arrival of Madam Malefic. "What do you make of our new neighbour?"

Hazel glanced up from a recipe book. Having had such a success with the stew, she now sought something more adventurous. "Seems we have a new contender for the title of village idiot."

"Mmm," muttered Belinda thoughtfully, "I recognised her as the woman I glimpsed when she almost ran me down in her carriage. She's taken Kryme Cottage. But something doesn't seem right." But there was no answer from Hazel as she scrutinised a recipe for Bouillabaisse.

***

The Bouillabaisse was not a success, but undeterred, Hazel had become a worshiper at the table of Edesia, the goddess of food. Various dishes found their way to the table or the waste bin. 'Why have I not discovered this before?' she asked herself. 'If I follow the recipe book, I can't go wrong. Well, maybe once or twice.' Now she had fantasies of a chain of discreet little cafes spread throughout the country – something like 'HAZEL'S, promising exquisite cuisine in exquisite surroundings, soft lighting, romantic music provided by a pianist (she could get students from various Music Academies for a song) but the highlight would always be her 'dish of the day'. There was also an ulterior motive behind this gastronomic paradigm, Quentin de La Tour. Learning from her fragrance mistake, she had consigned J'ai de la chance to the bottom drawer of her dresser and now wore nothing more potent than a dab of No:4711. It was her intention to let him see her as a domestic goddess with the promise her oven was the hottest he could find. The knock at the front door disturbed her reverie, and wiping her floury hands on her apron, she made her way along the hall.

On opening the door, she was face to face with Quentin. A flush of excitement filled her cheeks, and she raised a hand to pat her hair into place, thereby depositing several small lumps of incipient pastry. She smiled. Quentin frowned. "Oh, is Belinda at home?"

"No, she's with her parents." Hazel smiled even wider. "Won't you come in? I know I look a mess, but I'm making a Tourte Lorraine."

Quentin took a step back. "Err... not just now. I need to talk to her about something. The garden. Can you tell her to ring me the minute she gets home."

"My, that sound rather urgent," said Hazel flirtingly, "sure I can't help... in any way?"

Quentin took another step back. "No. Thanks. Just get her to call me." With that, he turned and walked back through the garden to the gate. He paused and glanced back.

Hazel was still standing at the door, the picture of marital bliss. "Will you join us for the pie tonight?"

He hurried out the gate and made his way home.

Chapter Six

"It's a wedding." Belinda had received Quentin's message from Hazel and was now walking around his undeveloped cottage garden with him. "It's an old friend of mine, and he's asked me to take the photographs," continued Quentin.

"When is it?" said Belinda, bending to look at some very early spring flower shoots.

"Christmas Eve."

Belinda straightened up. "Christmas Eve? That's an odd time to have a wedding."

Quentin shrugged. "I know, but they fly to New York on Christmas day. He starts a new job there, and the whole thing has been rushed so their parents and family could attend."

"Where are they getting married?"

"At St Mathew's down in Abbey Combe."

Belinda nodded. "So, what has it got to do with me?"

"I wondered if we could use your garden for some photographs. I can take some at the church, but these days they expect to have romantic photos of the bride and groom taken in dreamy settings."

"But my garden is bare at the moment, hardly dreamy. Some everlasting trees and shrubs but few flowers, very little colour."

"That's not a problem. They want black and white photos, and some of the bare trees will make an ideal setting."

Belinda nodded vacantly. She'd hardly heard Quentin's comments. "Have you had a visit from a woman from Kryme Cottage claiming to be Madam Malefic?"

Quentin gave a snort of derision. "Have I not. She turned up the other night, wanting me to attend a séance. Why? Has she invited you as well?"

Belinda nodded. "In a fashion. Don't worry, I won't be going. Hazel gave her short shrift."

"I can imagine," said Quentin with a smile as he imagined Hazel in full flight, dismissing the village's new arrival.

"I can't help thinking there is something odd about her," Belinda said as she inspected a budding bush.

"Odd! Try weird."

"No, I don't mean that. I know she's eccentric. I mean...well, I'm not sure what I mean. It's something I heard that's bugging me...and for the life of me, I can't remember what it is." She lapsed into thoughtful silence.

Quentin, realising he was forgotten, stopped and said, "So, is it OK to take the wedding photos in your garden?"

Belinda turned a blank face to him. "Wedding?"

***

Before Christmas, the remaining weeks saw Belinda entertaining her parents with some day trips to local beauty spots and a musical at the theatre. Each night they ate at the cottage and feasted on Hazel's newfound culinary treats, which promised to reach astronomical heights for Christmas Dinner. On Christmas Eve morning, Belinda and Hazel dressed in splendour, as Quentin had arranged for them to be his guests at his friend's wedding and breakfast. Belinda wanted Hazel's companionship as she would know no one else at the celebration, plus she wanted her to meet Charles and get her opinion of the new Vicar. After heavy rains overnight, the day had dawned overcast and grey but surprisingly warm. As they drove to Abbey Combe, both women were relaxed and ready to enjoy the day free from responsibilities and just enjoy the outing and the festivities.

The morning wedding ceremony set for eleven o'clock was brief. The bride and groom were soon posing in front of the Norman entry door, the only survivor of the original church after eager Victorian's converted it during their bizarre Early Gothic Revival frenzy. Guests were few, mainly immediate family members. Still, a succession of aunts and female cousins claimed many mandates to carry away photographic evidence of the union.

As Quentin, camera in hand, formed them into various groups, so each member of the suddenly united families was placated, Charles approached Belinda and Hazel. He had abandoned his liturgical splendour. Now, to the unknowing eye, he would pass for a London executive, dressed by Country Life, for a casual weekend away from the toils of the metropolis. "Well that went off smoothly, don't you think?" he said, "No one spoke up revealing any indiscretions that would have prevented the marriage. But I must say that indiscretions seem to be a badge of honour rather than an occasion for regret or a social handicap in this day and age."

"Hazel," said Belinda, with a grin, "let me introduce you to Charles Mead, our newly appointed vicar of Saint Mathew's."

Charles' eyes swung towards Hazel and, with a sweep up and down, returned to her face. "Well, *Hello*..." said Charles impiously. He took her hand. Hazel raised a questioning eyebrow. He sounded like an actor...a comic actor... Leslie Phillips in a Carry On film. I hope he doesn't say 'ding dong', she thought. She also pondered why her friend Belinda seemed so charmed by him. Handsome yes, but something...something...and of course, she could never be roomies with a Vicar. It would be like living in sin!

"Belinda didn't tell me she had such an attractive guest," said Charles, "one who she tells is preparing our sumptuous Christmas feast for tomorrow."

"That she is," said Belinda, amused by Charles' teasing of Hazel. She turned. "It looks as though the guests are getting ready to go to the pub for the wedding breakfast. Hazel, will you take the vicar along? I said I'd stay with Quentin while he took the photos in my garden."

"Oh," said Hazel quickly, "why don't you take the vicar...Charles... and I can look after Quentin."

"No, I know the garden better and can make some suggestions about settings for the photos." Inwardly Belinda laughed, as she picked up Quentin's camera case, aware Hazel wanted to spend some time alone with him. So a disgruntled Hazel was escorted off by Charles, who slid an arm around her waist. It took only a nanosecond for Hazel to free herself.

In the garden, the bride was busy checking her makeup for any damage caused by a heavenly blessing. The garden soil looked wet, possibly muddy, and she gave thanks that her veil was only shoulder length and her white wedding dress ended at her knee, so they would survive the garden. Not so her wedding shoes, which would be ruined. But as she'd borrowed them from cousin Lynn, it didn't matter too much. Anyway, Lynn, with five kids and another on the way, wouldn't be wanting them herself for another wedding.

The groom stood waiting, fiddling nervously with his tie. He hoped the photo session would be over soon; a pint at the pub was what he wanted. Quentin and Belinda emerged from some foliage and beckoned them.

Bride and groom began to pick their way across the sodden ground and were guided by Belinda to a small tree setting with bare white trunks creating a small grotto. Quentin placed them in the backdrop and commenced a search for the best angles to take shots. He began with a series of photos, each time directing the couple to various postures, supposedly to depict their eternal love for each other. The groom's thirst increased, the bride's annoyance at the muddy soil splattering her stockings. She hoped Quentin could erase the stains in the final photo.

"Let's try something different," said Quentin to the bride. "This time, step back a few paces and reach out to your husband, as though inviting him to join you." He raised his camera.

The bride took a few faltering steps backward and, as she raised her arm to her husband, it seemed as though the earth began to swallow her up. Indeed it was, and with a wail, the woman in white fell flat on her back in the mud.

Stunned, she gasped.

The gasp turned into a full-bodied scream.

For, close to her face, reaching out from the earth and dead leaves, a claw.

Decaying.

But still, a human hand.

Chapter Seven

To Belinda's mind, describing Christmas as a catastrophe was an understatement, although search as she may, she couldn't find a more appropriate turn of phrase. The bridal party had dissolved into recriminations, tears, mud, hysterics, and a delayed departure to New York.

Until late in the day, police had been interviewing Belinda and Hazel. The house and garden had been declared a crime scene, and forensic teams appropriated the grave and the corpse, while a police team made forays into the large garden for any clues that might aid in solving the crime. The gardeners who renovated the garden were to be interviewed, and housekeeper Mona Washington was recalled from Bristol, where she had gone to spend the holiday with her daughter. Lights had been set up around the burial place, and as night fell, the human remains were finally removed from the muddy grave and carried away for further analysis.

"It was a female," said Hazel, as she took a sip of her Walking Dead cocktail, "aged, I hear, about seventyish. Or so a young cop told me."

"Do they have any idea who she is?" said Belinda as she sank gratefully into an armchair. It had been an unforgettable and tiring day. Not to mention horrifying.

Hazel shrugged. "Not so far. And it may be difficult. Her face had been pretty well smashed in."

Belinda shuddered. "How horrible. But why?

Why in my garden? It doesn't make sense."

"The police think it was convenient the garden was under repair and made it easy for the murderers to ditch the body where any disturbed soil would go unnoticed."

"And I suppose the heavy rain washed some of it away, which is why... what's her name? The bride?...why she fell in."

Hazel finished her cocktail. "But whoever it was, knew about your garden works, so the murderer must be someone either locally or in Bath." She wandered to the window and peered at the young police officer on duty who was assigned to protect the crime site overnight. "It looks freezing out there. I wonder if the young constable would like something to warm him up. A cocktail perhaps? Maybe a Walking Dead?"

Belinda smiled to herself. No matter how awful a situation might be, Hazel could be relied on to stir the embers of lust. "Given that he's watching over the site of a recently emptied grave, perhaps something a little more cheerful?"

Hazel bit her lip in thought. "Yes... you're right. I'll make him a Flaming Fanny."

***

It was decided not to celebrate Christmas dinner at a site tinged with the recent recovery of a corpse; not only was it disrespectful but more than a little

Gothic, "Too close to M. R. James," said Hazel. Reluctantly they cancelled the date with Quentin and Charles and spent Christmas Day with Belinda's parents, who were full of questions about the murder, most of which Belinda couldn't answer. They attended Christmas Mass at the Abbey and enjoyed a pleasant meal at an hotel.

Quentin discovered an old girlfriend was visiting London and spent the day with her.

At the Vicarage Miss Atkins and Muriel Meldrew, on learning the Vicar was free for the day, tried to outdo each other in tempting him to their respective tables with an assortment of delicacies and homemade wines, which resulted in Charles suggesting they draw straws to settle the problem. This was done, and Muriel Meldrew drew the short straw and so carried her prize home. At the same time, Miss Atkins, with thunderous expression, ate plum pudding alone in her quarters of the Almshouses and drank several glasses of Elderberry wine, all under the judgmental eye of her cat, Beelzebub.

"And so," said Belinda's mother, "you don't have any idea who the poor soul is, or was I should say?"

Belinda sighed. She had been over all of this with her mother earlier, and there was nothing more she could add. "Mother, you know very well I was with you in Melbourne until a few weeks ago, so the whole thing is a mystery to me."

Mrs Lawrence looked unconvinced. "But

surely you have some thoughts on who the victim was. I mean, did she come from Milford? Is anyone missing from the village? Any new residents? Strangers, that sort of thing."

"Leave it off, mother. The police are investigating. They're holding the body in the morgue, so they will get all the answers eventually."

Mrs Lawrence wondered if that was the case. "Yes, but it happened in your village, in your garden. And I gather the poor woman's face had been disfigured, obviously to make it harder to identify her. Why did they do that?"

Belinda thought. Yes, why? Harder to identify the woman, agreed. But why? What was so special about the woman that the murderer had to ensure her identity was a mystery?

***

The drab winter days stretched on through January and into February. Belinda's parents, missing the Australian summer, fled to Melbourne, and life in Milford settled back, waiting for the stirring of Spring's vivacity. Police investigations into the murder of the mysterious woman had gone quiet, and life for Belinda and Hazel revolved around cosy days by the ever-present log fire, hurried forays to Bath for necessities, and Hazel's experimental kitchen triumphs – and disasters.

One late afternoon found Hazel toasting her

feet by the fire in the long room, the cottage's most cosy and comfortable chamber. One wall held a bookcase with volumes of Dickens, Thackeray, and Shakespeare, all gathered by Belinda's Great Aunt Jane. But more to Hazel's taste was the collection of first editions by the mystery writer, Ariadne Oliver, which revealed to Hazel the old woman had more mercurial tastes in literature than her display of the classics would indicate. As she reached for the last chocolate in the box, Hazel turned the page to the final chapter of Lady Don't Fall Backwards, where the detective had gathered all the suspects in the great hall of Mallison Mansion and was about to reveal the name of the murderer.

'I have gathered you all here to hear the result of my investigation of the murder of the Vicar of St Bartholomew's. I have found the murder weapon. The knife that was plunged so violently to terminate life.' He turned to face the woman seated in the shadows and held a bloody knife before her. 'Do you recognise this, Lady Fotherington Blyth Smythe?' Her ladyship blanched. The detective turned on his heel to face the assembly. 'But her Ladyship is not the murderer. The name of the killer is –'

"The reverend Charles... for you."

Hazel gave a start and was shocked from the imaginary world of Miss Oliver into the reality of Milford and Belinda standing before her, waving an envelope.

"It's from the Vicarage. Love letters from the clergy, is it?" said Belinda with a smile as she dropped the envelope into Hazel's lap. Still emerging from the fictional world, Hazel put the book aside, tore open the letter and began to read. "He wants me to come for dinner! At the vicarage!" She looked at Belinda in bewilderment. "Why?"

"Perhaps he wants to hear your sins," said Belinda grinning, as she opened another envelope. Reading the content, she frowned. "What do you make of this?" She passed the note to Hazel. "It's from that madwoman, Madam Malefic. She's invited us to a séance."

Hazel read the invitation aloud. "Madam Malefic invites you to an evening of mystical music and mesmerizing spirits, Thursday next at eight o'clock at Kryme Cottage." She looked at Belinda. "What makes you think it's a séance? Mesmerizing spirits might mean cocktails?"

Belinda took the note back from Hazel. "You live in hopes, don't you? See here, she signs herself as 'a spiritualist and poet, your mediator to the afterlife'. That can only mean a séance."

"But why would she invite us?"

"Maybe for the same reason the Vicar invites you to dinner."

"That being?"

"To get to know us better – or to find out what we know."

"About what?"

"To pick our brains. There's been a murder, and it took place here in my garden. She's just being nosey, or..."

"Or what? You think-?"

"She is guilty? And wants to know if we suspect her ?" Belinda shook her head. "Well, there is no evidence to suggest that. Still, the séance would give us a chance to learn more about Madam Malefic. And there is that other matter."

"What's that?" said Hazel.

"The matter of the missing reverend Lamb."

"Hmmm....Mona tells me the police have reported another sighting of him in Exeter. He gets about, doesn't he?"

***

The black lace cover was removed from the round table as Belinda took her place. She was joined by Hazel and Quentin. After some persuasion, Belinda had convinced them that Madam Malefic's attempt to communicate with spirits, would allow them to study this mysterious woman. Even if the spooks were unwilling, it might provide some laughs on a cold winter night. Not that the interior of Kryme Cottage was warm; Belinda felt the ancient stone walls and floor welcomed the icy blasts and stored them as a miser would store golden coins.

Hazel shivered and sunk further into her voluminous woollen coat. "So, where's this madam Arcarti?" In answer to her question, the figure of the man who had admitted them materialised beside her. Belinda recognised him to be the person had been standing behind Madam Malefic the night she had first called at her cottage. He was dressed in black and still had a vaguely cowered posture. He smelled of peppermint.

"I am Madam's nephew. Madam will be with you shortly," he said timidly. He then placed three candles on the table and lit the wicks before blending back into the shadows.

"At last, some warmth," said Hazel sardonically.

The interior of the cottage's main room had changed little from Belinda's previous stolen visit; some rugs of violent design covered the uneven floor. Several paintings of a transcendental nature hung on the walls, plus a copy of the sketch of Jane Austen by her sister and closest friend, Cassandra. A motley collection of worn Victorian furniture looked lost in the vast space. Two electric lights stands provided little illumination in the sombre atmosphere of the darkened room.

Belinda leaned to Quentin and whispered. "Thanks for agreeing to bring us here tonight. It might be a waste of your time."

Quentin smiled and squeezed her hand. "Try and stop me. I'm just as curious as you about our new neighbour, particularly one who dashes around the town by horse and carriage."

The distant sound of footsteps and creaking wood reminded Belinda of the staircase leading up to the room with the small wooden cupboard.

It was from the staircase that the dark figure

of Madam Malefic emerged and sauntered towards her guests. As usual, she was dressed all in black, her dress festooned with elaborate black lace and a matching mantilla draped over her head and shoulders. Silently she placed a plate containing slices of rich chocolate cake on the table.

Hazel sat up. "Oooh, choccie cake." She reached to take a piece, but Madam Malefic darted forward and slapped her hand. "The food is for the spirits." Chastened, Hazel slid back into her chair.

Madam Malefic took her place at the remaining seat and surveyed her guests. "I should warn you that the spirits can sense the presence of sceptics." She turned a critical eye towards Hazel. "They can harm the séance's chances of success." Feeling that she had cowed Hazel's provincialism, she said to Belinda, "If you have no objection, I suggest we try and contact your Great Aunt, Miss Jane Lawrence."

Belinda gave a start. "Oh! I hadn't thought..."

Madam Malefic shook her head gently, "Never fear. She will not be disturbed, and will only come through if she wishes to." She turned aside to her nephew. "Darcy, turn out the lights."

In a swell of peppermint, Darcy did as he was bid, and the room was in total darkness apart from the three flickering candles. "I want you now to hold hands in a circle. Hold them tight." Madam reached out to Belinda and Hazel, who were on her left and right. Her hands were icy cold but held their fingers in a vice-like grip. Belinda glanced at Quentin as she took his hand. She was beginning to feel uncomfortable at the prospect of raising Aunt Jane's phantom. Quentin took Hazel's other hand as she vainly tried to ease Madam's grip.

"Silence!" commanded Madam in a robust and loud voice. The three ceased their activities and, with eyes turned to Madam, waited in silence for whatever was to come. As though used to the ritual and playing his part, Darcy switched on a record player and gently lowered the needle onto the vinyl disc. Scratchy sound filled the room, and eventually, a reedy voice began to sing. A female voice.

Madam closed her eyes and began in a soft high pitched childlike way to gently hum along with the recorded version, 'We'll meet again... don't know where...'

Hazel tried to cover a snort of amusement, the singer was no Vera Lynn, but felt Madam's fingers tighten on hers, to the point that she almost cried out in pain. After a nerve-wracking two minutes, the ghostly singing came to an end. Madam broke off the humming and spoke in a deep, hard voice. "Oh cherished Jane Lawrence, we bring you offerings from life into death." She cast wintry eyes towards the chocolate cake. "Commune with us, Jane Lawrence, and advance among us."

There was a long silence with only the slight patter of rain on the roof. The candles fluttered in a sudden cold breeze, and Belinda shivered not from the chill, but the tense atmosphere.

Again in a deep but louder voice, Madam repeated the request. Still, there was silence. The three glanced at each other in the dark, each wondering what would happen next. Madam sank back into her chair. In a low voice, she said, "I...I don't think.." Her voice faded, then she slumped forward and asked in a deep masculine voice. "Jane? Is that you?... Jane..." She nodded and gave a crooked smile.

Belinda glanced at Quentin. Was Madam actually conjuring up her Aunt's spirit?

Madam gave a light laugh and continued almost in a conversational manner, "Jane... you must tell me... I know... There is the power of white lace... the potency of lace. There is the black lace...a shroud, worn against death... for death." She gave a titter. "The black lace-topped stocking...drives most men absolutely wild...sophisticated seduction. Nothing aids the art of seduction more...a hint of black lace. But tell me...tell me of your Aunt...I implore you!"

She fell into silence, her head on her chest. Unexpectedly she woke, and glanced around at the others. "Did she speak? Did she tell you?"

Belinda said softly, "My Aunt? I don't know. You were talking to *a* Jane...but nothing made sense. You talked about lace."

Madam sat erect. "Lace? You heard only me?" The three nodded in agreement. Madam sank back, seemingly disappointed. "The wrong Jane." Distressed, she looked about her. "I can't go on again tonight. Captain Frederick, the lights!" A large near neanderthal, previously unseen by the group, emerged from the dark, and the Captain did as he was bid, returning the room to its previous murky hollow. He glowered at the visitors making his dislike plain for all to see.

Madam stood. "I'm afraid I must ask you to leave. It has exhausted me."

The others rose. Hazel reached out and snatched a piece of the cake. "If the spooks don't want this, I do," and wolfed down what was to have been a spiritual feast.

"Well, what was that all about?" said Quentin, as he started the engine and drove his car back to Belinda's cottage.

"It's a mystery to me," said Belinda. "If she was talking to *my* Aunt Jane, why was she asking her about *her* Aunt?"

"Did she have one?"

"I'm sure she probably did have, but don't know who it was. I don't have a family tree. And why would Madam want to contact her?"

"Perhaps she lived in Kryme Cottage at one time," said Hazel from the back seat,
"you know, talk to the spirits who lived there."

"Possibly, but why?" said Belinda.

"Maybe to find out about a secret."

"What secret?" said Quentin.

"How the hell should I know," said Hazel, harshly, "I'm just guessing. I'm curious to know more of Captain Whatshisname...Frederick?""

Belinda was thoughtful. "And all that talk about lace? My aunt Jane wasn't into lace, as far as I know."

"So maybe this Jane wasn't your Aunt, but

someone else?" said Quentin, as he drew the car to a stop at the cottage.

"Well, I'm with the old Madam on one thing, said Hazel, licking the residue of chocolate frosting from her fingers.

"Oh? And what's that?" said Belinda.

"Black lace-topped stockings. Works every time for me."

Chapter Eight

Hazel gave a cavernous yawn as she entered the long room. A cup of steaming coffee perfumed the morning air. To her surprise, Belinda was seated near the fire sifting through the contents of a battered suitcase. Without looking up, she said, "I sent an email to my father, asking if he knew anything about Aunt Jane having an Aunt."

"And?" said Hazel, settling at the other side of the fire.

"Still waiting for a reply. But I thought I'd look through Aunt Jane's bits and bobs that I kept after her funeral. So far, I've got seven recipes for marmalade and two for Bubble and Squeak. But no sign of who would be, to me, a Great, Great Aunt? Would that be right?"

"Haven't a clue. But listen, Bel. Tonight I'm to have dinner at the vicarage with Charles..."

Belinda sat back in her chair. "Yes. What about it?"

Hazel squirmed. "Well, I don't fancy being alone with him."

"Why not?"

"He's a vicar, and frankly, he makes me feel uncomfortable."

Belinda smiled. "Frightened he will try to cure you of your wicked ways"?

Hazel ignored the jibe. "No, it's not that. He's just a bit too touchy feely."

"You never complained before about men like that."

Hazel gave a nod of agreement. "But this time, it's a clergyman. So I want you to come with me."

"But I haven't been invited."

"No matter. He'll be too much of a gentleman to refuse you. Be ready by seven-thirty." She rose and walked to the door. "By the way, have you seen that book I was reading? A mystery, Lady Don't Fall Backwards. I can't find it anywhere."

Belinda shook her head and resumed searching through the suitcase.

"I was just about to find out who the murderer was," said Hazel crossly, as in a vain attempt of finding the book, she flipped a cushion aside on the settee.

***

Promptly at eight o'clock, Hazel rang the bell at the Vicarage door. Belinda lagged a little behind her, still not convinced that Charles would welcome her presence. Secretly she was delighted at the opportunity of being close to him again. A moment later, the door swung open, and a beaming host smiled a welcome to Hazel. The smile melted as she moved forward, and Belinda was revealed, "I hope you don't mind, Charles, but I've brought Belinda along."

Charles hurriedly substituted his smile,

although this time with not so much ardour. "Of course. Welcome, Belinda." He ushered the women in, taking their coats while wondering if the steak and kidney pie would stretch three ways. As he hung the coats on a hall stand, Belinda noticed a large key rack nearby. Of cumbersome Victorian design it displayed keys of all shapes and sizes, antiquated, heavy and solid, new, all hung in regimented order, each bearing a label, 'vestry'. 'choir'. 'church door'. The last one was a bright new silver key and simply labelled 'K'. Kitchen? thought Belinda

Leading the way to the dining room, Charles called out, "Miss Atkins! Muriel!" His welcoming arm slid around Hazel's waist before quickly sliding down. Hazel gave a slight yelp and pushed him away.

The dining table had been set for two, with candles and fresh flowers as a centre piece. The lighting was low while a Tudor love song on the CD player asserted,

Much ado there was, God wot!
He would love, and she would not:
She said, never man was true:
He said, none was false to you.
He said, he had loved her long:
She said, love should have no –

Charles quickly switched off the player and turned the lights up fully. Miss Atkins and Muriel Meldrew appeared in the doorway, their eyes wide at the unexpected visitor's presence.

"Ladies, as you can see, I have an extra guest. I trust

this won't upset your culinary arrangements?"

The two women began to whisper urgently into each other's ear while casting an occasional critical look at the offending guest. Belinda watched them, and it occurred to her they resembled wafer-thin versions of two spinster aunts in a film she'd seen years ago.

It being decided there was enough food for the evening, Belinda and Hazel took their place at the table while Charles foraged around to supply Belinda with cutlery. She watched in amusement as he poured the wine, spilling some of it. Due to her unexpected arrival, his usual poise deserted him, and his romantic evening with Hazel was abandoned. She liked him now, lacking his usual savoir-faire, and admitted to herself he was very handsome and charming.

The evening proceeded and the food delicious. Belinda began to feel like a fifth wheel, as Charles devoted his time almost exclusively to Hazel. During a short break in his act of adoration, Belinda claimed his attention. "You're lucky to have your two acolytes so devoted to you."

Charles, still beneath Hazel's allure, reluctantly turned to her. "Hmmm? What? Oh, you mean Miss Atkins and Muriel? Yes, they have taken me under their wing, so to speak. Can't do enough for me. Treat me like the son they never had, I suppose. Between you and me, I call them Heckle and Jeckle, not to their face, I mean." He gave a boyish snigger.

In the kitchen, in an atmosphere of disquiet,

Heckle and Jeckle were preparing coffee and petit fours. "He's started bringing women home," said Miss Atkins, as she switched on the coffee grinder. The noise of the blades cutting into the hard beans reflected her mood.

Muriel placed the cakes on a silver platter. "Yes. And I don't like the way he is paying so much attention to that piece of mutton dressed as lamb."

"You mean, the Whitby woman?" said Miss Atkins, as she switched off the machine and proceeded with the coffee preparation. "She's no better than she should be. But you're right. We don't want predatory females chasing after him, not after all we do, and have done."

Muriel adjusted the white apron over her black dress and patted her silver hair into place. "We agreed not to talk about that. We should just be thankful our prayers were answered. Our task now is to see that the reverend behaves in an exemplary manner and brings St Mathew's qualities to the attention of Lambeth Palace."

Charles led Belinda and Hazel into the comfortable lounge where they seated themselves. "Coffee will be along soon," said Charles, as he placed another log on the fire.

Belinda sank back into the cushions. "Charles, when I first met you, we talked about the reverend Lamb, who was to have been the vicar here. Has he been found?"

Charles shook his head. "No. As I told you, there were one or two supposed sightings in Chelsea and one in Wells. So, still listed as a missing person."

Belinda held her hands towards the heat of the fire. "It does seem odd."

Hazel, relieved the pressure from Charles was off her, rose and inspected the large bookcase, the contents of which were mostly religious essays and Church law. She heard Belinda and Charles continue their discussion, but the matter was no concern to her as she flipped through the contents of a heavy leather-bound volume.

"Did we tell you we attended a séance the other night?" said Belinda.

Charles was surprised. "A séance? Don't tell me I've fallen into a nest of mystics?"

Belinda gave a laugh. "I doubt it. It was just Madame Malefic."

Charles looked bewildered. "Madam Malefic? I wouldn't have thought it. She is such a sweet old biddie. Roses and violets, that sort of thing."

Before Belinda could respond, the door opened, and Miss Atkins and Muriel entered bearing aromatic coffee and the icing covered cakes.

As she was about to return to her seat, Hazel saw a paperback novel on a chair. She picked it up and read out the title, "Lady don't fall backwards!"

Charles looked at her. "Oh, that's just a murder mystery Miss Atkins gave me to read. I haven't started it."

"I've been reading it but seem to have misplaced my copy."

"Take it, by all means, I'm sure Miss Atkins will not object."

Muriel and Miss Atkins glanced at him and then at each other. Hazel saw the glance and put the book down. "No matter. I'll have a good look for it at the cottage. It must be there." She took her seat, and Muriel, her hand shaking a little, poured the coffee. Some dark drops landed on Hazel's dress. Uncharacteristically, Hazel did not immediately dismember Muriel; only her eyes revealed she was writing the woman's obituary.

***

"After the séance, I remember you said, 'maybe this Jane wasn't your aunt, but someone else?'" said Belinda. She and Quentin were in Bath walking along Lower Borough Walls on the way to SouthGate precinct. "I've been thinking about that, but I can't imagine who it would be."

Quentin took her arm as they crossed the road. "Maybe she just got a crossed line, rang your Aunt, and got another Jane."

"No, she specifically said, 'tell me of your Aunt', so she apparently got through to the person she wanted. She wouldn't ask if it was some unidentified spirit she'd called up."

"Whoever it was, seemed to be important to Madam. Calling up her spirit and rabbiting on about lace."

"Yes. Lace. It seems especially important to Madam. It covers everything she wears."

They reached SouthGate Place and made their way through the shoppers until Quentin stopped at a photographic store. "This is the place I want."

Belinda looked in the window at the display of cameras. "What are you looking for?"

Quentin pulled a brochure from his pocket. "I'm buying a Drone."

"What on earth for?" asked Belinda as she peered at the pamphlet.

"I can take photos or videos. It will be a great help to me. Getting the camera up so high for landscapes which otherwise I couldn't do."

"Well, if you say so," said Belinda impartially.

"It might take a while. Do you want to come with me?"

"Er...no. I'll browse, have a coffee, then head home." Belinda pointed to a cafe nearby.

Quentin gave the 'thumbs up' and eagerly entered the store. Belinda began a slow walk around the square, stopping now and then to window shop. The fashion houses were featuring their Spring Collections, and she mentally saw herself wearing bright colours the designers had decreed as faux haute couture, for those who could only afford ready-to-wear.

She passed on and came to a fabric store with a display of William Morris draperies. The materials would be ideal for recovering a settee in the long room. Admiring them, she entered the shop and picked up a fabric swatch book. The shop attendant was dealing with a truculent customer.

"I'm sorry, madam, you've seen everything we have." The frustration in her voice caused Belinda to turn and was surprised to see a familiar figure talking to the saleswoman. A figure dressed in black. It was Madam Malefic.

"Well, I've been wasting my time, it seems," said Madam indignantly, "and I was told you would be able to help me. Good afternoon!" So saying she turned and in a rage stalked from the shop, indignation blinding her to Belinda's presence.

The attendant gave a sigh. "I'm sorry you had to witness that. I tried to explain to her that we were unable to supply what she required."

Belinda moved to the counter. "Oh, what was that?"

"Lace."

Belinda smiled. "Ha, that comes as no surprise."

"And it wasn't just any lace. What she wanted was fourteenth century Irish lace! I ask you? Did she think she could walk in off the street and just pick up six hundred year old lace? I told her she should try the V and A. Old lace indeed," the woman concluded huffily.

"Yes, I know her, and she does have a passion for lace. She lives in my village at Kryme Cottage. Just recently moved there. She's Madam Malefic."

The attendant frowned. "No, I think you've

made a mistake."

"Why?"

"Well," said the attendant, as she began to pack away lace samples, "the lady gave her name as Mrs Jane Leigh Perrot."

Chapter Nine

"Fake! I knew it. Fake!" declared Hazel, as she placed raspberries in the bottom of six ramekins. She had invited Quentin to dinner and was in the final stages of preparing raspberry and lavender Crème Brûlée. Belinda removed her coat and tossed it over the back of a chair. "Obviously. But why? Why call herself Madam Malefic if she is really Mrs Perrot?

"A fake name for her fake act as a spiritualist," said Hazel, straining a cream and egg mixture through a sieve.

"Possibly," muttered Belinda as she distractedly took a raspberry from a ramekin and popped it into her mouth. Hazel glared at her and moved the ramekins out of her reach. "But on the other hand, she may be Madam Malefic and, for some reason or other, wants to be known as Mrs Perrot."

"Whoever she is," said Hazel.

"True."

"Malefic is just some old crank and best we forget about her and have nothing to do with her," said Hazel, as she poured the cream over the raspberries.

"Maybe. I've just thought of something. When I first visited Charles at the vicarage, he mentioned he'd met Madam and thought she would probably be polishing the church brass or arranging flowers along with Atkins and Meldew, his two devotees. Plus, he called her a sweet old biddie."

"And?" said Hazel as she placed the ramekins into a bain-marie.

"Think about it. Can you see Madam Malefic on her knees in the church polishing brass, or sticking flowers into vases."

Hazel was about to place the bain-marie into the oven when a faint buzzing sound made her pause. She looked out the window and from the pub down the hill, and racing up high over the garden towards the cottage, was a strange object. Belinda joined her at the window. The object was travelling at a fast rate and was soon near the cottage. It continued on, growing closer and closer. The buzzing noise increased, and with a startling crash, the object struck the window.

The window cracked.

A drone fell to the ground.

Hazel dropped the bain-marie.

There would be no raspberry and lavender Crème Brûlée that night.

"I'm lucky only one of the four rotor blades got damaged," said Quentin as he inspected the offending drone. I'll have to take it back and see if I can get it repaired."

"And learn how to use it," said Belinda with a smile. Hazel was not so forgiving. She viewed her neighbour with censorious eyes. But her attraction to the handsome male won over any grumpiness, and she decided that his punishment in ruining her Crème Brûlée would be mild. He could clean up the mess he had created.

"Yes," said Quentin in reply to Belinda, "there are all kinds of rules and regulations, and I have to register the drone before using it for photography. Sorry about your window. I'll pay for the repairs."

Belinda glanced at the cracked pane. "It's pretty old and was due to be replaced anyway. How soon can you get the drone repaired?"

Quentin shrugged. "Not sure, but I'll let you know. Why do you ask?"

"Oh, just an idea I have. I'll tell you more when the drone can fly again."

***

"Kryme cottage? It has been sold." Mr Abernathy (of Abernathy & Ffrench, Estate Agents & Property Consultants proud sponsor of the Bath Syllabub Festival) peered over his pince-nez at the antipodean and her brash English companion.

"Yes, we know," said Belinda, wondering how Mr Abernathy's tailor managed to almost recreate Dickensian clothing, which the estate agent obviously favoured. This eccentricity became complete with the appearance of a small silver box from which the elderly Abernathy selected a pinch of snuff and sniffed some of the ground up tobacco leaves into each nostril. "We were wondering if you could tell us about the new owner, Madam Malefic?" continued Belinda.

The agent produced a large silk handkerchief, and flinging it over his nose, snuffled loudly into it. "Madam Malefic, you say? Can't say I can." He turned to a middle-aged woman seated at a typewriter. "Miss Woodhouse, the Kryme cottage sale?"

In her fluffy pink twin set and pearls, hoary Miss Woodhouse reached for a small wooden file and flicked through well-worn cards. Hazel doubted the pearls' provenance and wondered how the woman coped with spending her days in this one tiny office with the peculiar Mr Abernathy. Was she his office squeeze? The evidence seemed doubtful. The dark and dusty panelled room was barely big enough for the two of them and suggested the better days of trading for Abernathy and Ffrench were behind them. Miss Woodhouse selected one card and silently passed it to Mr Abernathy, who peered closely at the handwritten record. "Ah, yes. The sale was negotiated by Major Ffrench."

"Can we talk with him," asked Hazel.

Mr Abernathy paused, frozen for the moment as though about to sneeze. But the irritation passed, and he resumed some mobility. "I'm afraid not. The Major is retired now and living in Scotland. He is of an advanced age, you understand, and has no contact now with the outside world. An isolated man who sadly does not appreciate his good fortune in discarding society." He turned to Miss Woodhouse. "Do you have any recollection of this Madam Malefic?"

Miss Woodhouse replied in so low a voice it

caused Belinda and Hazel to lean forward until they were almost face to face with the woman. "You will recall, Mr Abernathy, the property had been owned by an American gentleman, from Schenectady, it seems. He had inherited the property years ago on the death of his great uncle. The gentleman himself had been confined to a lunatic asylum for many years. It wasn't until his passing, at age one hundred and five, due I'm told, to a fall from the asylum observation tower, which he had climbed in the erroneous conviction that the British were coming, that the property was placed on the market. The sale of the cottage could not take place until his estate had been settled. Major Ffrench dealt with it all through his legal compatriots, so the new owner, this Madam Malefic, never set foot in this office."

With no clear identification of Madam Malefic, the disappointed women clambered down the worn staircase from the top floor of the once residential building, now converted to offices and a dismal second-hand book shop. Nearby, a flea market was closing up for the day, but Hazel, ever on the lookout for an undiscovered Titian or at least a George III silver spoon, propelled Belinda towards it.

"If Charles is right," said Belinda, "and the woman he met as Madam Malefic was made of lavender and roses, that means –"

"That means," interrupted Hazel, as she picked over a motley collection of fish knives, "the real Madam Malefic, after a sojourn in your garden, is in the morgue awaiting identification."

"And this Mrs Perrot killed her and took her place. To get Kryme Cottage? If so, what's so special about the cottage that she is prepared to kill for?"

They mulled over this question as they continued back along Gay Street. It was a distinct possibility, but they could hardly tell the police their suspicions without any firm evidence. Passing the Jane Austin Centre Belinda grasped Hazel by the arm. "Look!" The object that caught her attention was a poster.

An afternoon with Jane & Oscar
Madam Malefic presents readings from
the works of Jane Austen & Oscar Wilde.
Theatre Royal.

"Those wishing to audition please ring Madam Malefic," read Belinda. A mobile phone number completed the advertisement.

"Good grief," said Hazel as they walked on, "the woman is pushy. She no doubt thinks herself a combination of Henry Irving and Lillie Langtry, reincarnated."

"Probably," said Belinda, "but you and I are going to audition."

Hazel stopped in her tracks. "Have you lost what little reason you do have?"

"Think about it. It will give us a chance to be near her and find out as much as we can if we're to consider her a murderer."

Hazel looked doubtful. "Maybe, but there must be other ways."

"What? Eternally inviting her to tea and crumpets? No. My plan is subtler and likely to succeed if we can win her over. Besides, you might get a leading role, with press coverage, rave notices, star treatment." Even though Belinda doubted such kudos, to Hazel, it raised a spark of dormant ego. She was already composing her acceptance speech as she received her Olivier Award from a Judi or a Maggie's admiring hands.

***

"But you'd make a perfect Jack Worthing," said Belinda as she added cream to her coffee, "if they do a reading from The Importance." She and Hazel had returned to Milford and decided as there appeared to be two Madam Malefic's, one real and dead, one fake and a murderer, to avoid confusion, they would refer to the fake one as Madam Perrot.

Full of ideas on how they could reveal Madam Perrot as a murderer with their plans to audition for the forthcoming theatrical afternoon, they were trying to convince Quentin to join them. Although she wouldn't admit it, Hazel was also seeking ways to spend more time with Quentin and this seemed an artful way of doing it. Quentin, unaware of the hidden agenda, was not so keen on treading the boards. "Me? On stage? No, thanks." He laughed as he sat down opposite the two women who had arrived breathless at his door late in the afternoon.

Hazel leaned forward and tapped him on the knee, allowing her fingers to remain for a tantalising moment. "There's no doubt you'd be chosen. You have everything an actor needs. Good looks, charm, virility."

Quentin flushed and scratched his knee, where Hazel's fingers had lingered. "No, thanks. I'd make a fool of myself. Besides, I'll be away. I'll be in London for a while on a photo assignment. Tourist promotion stuff."

"Right," said Belinda. "Cards on the table. We suspect that this Madam Malefic, who we believe is actually a Mrs Jane Leigh Perrot, murdered the real Madam and buried her in my garden."

"Oh? Proof? said Quentin, relieved the talk of acting had ended.

"We have none," said Belinda. "That's why we want to attend the auditions and hopefully the play readings, so we can ingratiate ourselves with this Madam or Mrs or whatever, and get clues that confirm our suspicions."

"And find out why she wants the cottage so desperately," added Hazel, who's fingers again found Quentin's knee. She was disappointed as Quentin rose quickly and warmed his hands by the fire. "What makes you think the body belonged to this real Madam Malefic?"

"It seems odd there is a missing woman, and suddenly there is a buried female corpse. The two go together," said Belinda.

"But what evidence do you have there is or was a missing woman."

"The vicar... Charles, he met her after she bought the cottage," said Belinda, "and he described her as being just a sweet old lady."

"Maybe his idea of a sweet old lady fits Madam Malefic's description," said Quentin with a smile.

"Be serious," said Hazel.

"All I'm saying is, you only have one man's description of the woman. If I were you, I'd have a chat with the vicar's disciples."

"Disciples?" said Hazel, standing to join him by the fire.

Quentin gently edged away and poured a fresh cup of coffee. "Those two you tell me about, who do the church flowers...Mrs...?"

"Miss Atkins and Muriel Meldrew," said Belinda.

***

"Yes, madam. Of course. Thank you." Muriel Meldrew put down the phone and walked into the kitchen. Miss Atkins looked up from slicing apples.

"Who was that?"

"Need you ask? It was her. She insists we attend the auditions she's holding for her afternoon readings at the Theatre Royal."

Miss Atkins sighed. "I do wish she'd leave us alone! It goes on and on and on." She turned from the apples and walked to the Almshouse window and looked towards the vicarage.

Muriel took over the apples and placed them in the prepared pastry. "We both know there is no chance of that." She put the pastry lid on the pie. "Not unless..."

Miss Atkins turned to her. "Well, we could try. After all, we do have –"

Muriel cut her short. "Now is not the time. Let things be, for the moment." She placed the pie in the oven. "What have you prepared for the reverend tonight?"

Miss Atkins threw off her apron in a fit of frustration. "Lamb chops. He's been trying to ring that woman all day."

"Did he speak to her? What did he say?" asked Muriel.

"She didn't answer. He left messages."

Muriel nodded. "She and Belinda were out. I saw them walking in Gay street."

Miss Atkins looked concerned. "What if he wants to marry her?"

Muriel nodded. "Just keep your eye on him and report what he does. And as for him marrying, we both know the answer to that."

***

Charles lay down his knife and fork and licked some mint jelly from his finger. He frowned as he thought back over the day and how Miss Atkins has been so annoying. Every time he turned around there she was, dusting or polishing. Most unnerving. It was almost as though she was spying on him. He was also annoyed that Hazel had not returned his calls. He picked up his phone and checked it, but received no joy. A pointless exercise as he knew he would be disappointed. Once again, he wondered if he had done the right thing in accepting the ministry in Abbey Combe. It was so isolated, parochial, even with Bath so nearby. The attendances at Evensong were few and far between, and he wondered if anyone would know or care if he cancelled it. He took up a flyer that has been in the mail with a request for it to be posted on the church's noticeboard.

An afternoon with Jane & Oscar
Madam Malefic presents readings from
the works of Jane Austen & Oscar Wilde.
Theatre Royal.

An amused grin was his reaction. Madam Malefic seemed an unlikely theatrical impresario. Small, slight, and grey-haired. Just like someone's elderly grandmother. However, some waters run deep, and the old lady might have hidden talents. But he brightened at the thought of Kryme cottage. He hadn't seen Madam Malefic since the day she called on him all those months ago. Now that she had taken up residence there, he had legitimate reasons to call on her, but until he was sure of his facts, planned clandestine visits were necessary. He reached for the dish of apple pie, took a mouth full, and immediately grimaced. Miss Atkins must have forgotten to add sugar. It was very bitter.

***

Belinda and Hazel arrived at the Theatre Royal and were met at the door by Darcy. He handed them a sheaf of papers and gave directions to the rehearsal room. "If you'll just fill in your names and contact details, plus any acting experience you may have." A few other locals arrived, all anticipating an amusing Saturday afternoon and possibly a free tea. As they made their way through the theatre, Belinda said. "Have you had any acting experience?"

Hazel looked thoughtful. "Yes, as a matter of fact."

"Where and when?"

"If you'll be patient, you'll find out," said Hazel, pushing open the door to the rehearsal room. A group of theatre enthusiasts, local and some from surrounding villages, sat in a semi-circle around Madam. Mainly middle-aged women with one or two teenage girls, and a handful of willowy males. Belinda was surprised to see Miss Atkins and Muriel attending a tea urn nearby.

Madam, dressed in her customary black lace, rose to greet them. "I'm glad you both came. I was hoping you would." She laid a firm hand on Hazel's arm. "You are the perfect Lady Bracknell, and I won't have you say a word against it." She thrust two worn and slightly greasy copies of The Importance of Being Earnest into Hazel's hand, "Page twenty-six, the handbag scene." Casting a jaundiced eye over the few males in the group, she added, "You'd be advised to find a man to play Jack." Turning to Belinda, she said, "And for you, my pretty, Jane Austen. I've marked some poems, but I left them at the cottage, careless of me. Rehearsal here next Saturday at one o'clock sharp. Don't be late." With that, Madam turned back to the group, "Now, is anyone skilled in Dickens? I need a male and a female reader."

Dismissed as they were, Belinda and Hazel ventured into Westgate Street in a daze. The whirlwind visit to the theatre and the fact Madam Perrot had anticipated their attendance, with works already selected for them to perform, was unexpected. "How did she know we'd even come today?" asked Hazel.

"Perhaps the spirits told her," said Belinda with a smile.

"The woman is weird."

"No argument there. But if you're to play Lady Bracknell, who will be playing opposite you as Jack Worthing?" said Belinda.

"I wouldn't trust her choice. Quentin is ideal, but he doesn't want to, "said Hazel in a disappointed voice.

"What about Charles?"

"I'd rather not," said Hazel, recalling his wandering hands.

"But he'd be perfect, and I'm sure he'd enjoy it. I'll call him and put the idea to him," said Belinda, chuckling to herself. It was another opportunity to spend some time with Charles.

***

"I've got something to show you," said Quentin excitedly. Belinda and Hazel had barely returned home from the meeting with Madam Perrot when Quentin knocked forcefully on their door. Once admitted, he waved a Tablet at them. "I've been experimenting with the drone, and what I've found will knock your socks off."

"I haven't worn socks since I was in kindergarten," said Hazel.

Quentin ignored her. "I was experimenting with the video camera on the drone and sent it off in the direction of Abbey Combe. It was going well until I passed by Kryme cottage." He switched on the tablet and waited for a video to appear. "I've transferred down the video I took, and just you look and see..."

The others crowded around to look at the screen. After a few rocky starts, the drone took off and showed an image taken from Quentin's garden. It rose high up over the village, turned, and proceeded along the path Belinda knew so well. "This is where it gets exciting," said Quentin.

Belinda's eyes were fixed on the screen. The view from up high was pretty, despite the wintery setting. The drone rose up above trees with Kryme cottage coming into view. Belinda looked closer. The was a figure, a man, entering the garden and walking confidently to the front door. He paused, took keys from his pocket, unlocked the door, and entered.

"But... that's Charles!" said Belinda in amazement.

"'told you, you be surprised," said Quentin.

The image moved on and came to an end. "I had to bring it home," said Quentin, "it was running out of power."

"But did Charles leave the cottage?" said Hazel

"More importantly, what was he doing there," said Belinda. "He had a key. Why would Madam Perrot give him a key?"

Chapter 10

Belinda slept poorly that night as a million questions swirled in her mind. Charles had claimed not to have seen Madam since she had taken up residence in the cottage, yet the video evidence revealed he must have had some contact with her; otherwise, how did he come to be in possession of the keys?

Did he know that Madam Perrot was absent and in Bath at the time he visited? And how long had he been in contact with her? To have given him the keys, she must have trusted him. Was he telling the truth when he said he'd only seen the woman once? And if that were the case, it was highly unlikely that she would have given him keys on her first casual meeting.

And his description of her, roses, and violets. An old biddy, he called her. None of it made sense. She would talk to Hazel in the morning and convince her she must have Charles play opposite her as Jack Worthing. That way, they could gauge his closeness with Madam Perrot.

Pleased that she had a plan of action, she settled down under the duvet, but sleep still alluded her, and the whole mystery began again to endlessly unwind in her mind.

***

"Don't tell him we have the video of him at Kryme cottage," said Belinda, as she and Hazel approached the vicarage. "I want to get his reaction when he meets Madam Perrot. If he doesn't recognise her, it confirms that this Mrs Perrot has murdered the real Madam Malefic and taken her place." She knocked on the door.

"Alright," said Hazel, "but I'm still not keen on him playing Jack. Couldn't we try asking Quentin again?"

Charles opened the door. He looked less like a vicar than a sportsman fresh from a game of golf.

"Good morning," said Belinda, feeling a rush of pleasure at the sight of him. Silently she wished he would be playing another scene in The Importance, one with Gwendolyn, a role she felt she was suited for. "We've come on a mission. Madam Malefic is holding auditions for a play and poetry reading, we're performing, and we would like you to join us."

Charles gave a laugh. "Yes, I saw that. But what makes you think I can act?"

"What makes you think we can," said Hazel.

Charles's smile broadened as he turned to her. "I'm sure the critics will be at your feet, but I don't think the public is ready to see me performing before them."

"Nonsense," said Hazel, "you do that every Sunday."

Belinda felt that Hazel wasn't helping, and

Charles was about to refuse the request, so decided to use subterfuge and lie. "It's for a charity, so I think you should reconsider."

"Oh, charity? Which one?"

"Um...er...the 'save the hairy nosed wombats', isn't that so, Hazel?"

Hazel looked blank.

"And you be playing opposite Hazel in the handbag scene from The Importance," said Belinda, hoping that would sweeten the deal. It did.

Charles's eyes lit up, and he gazed at Hazel. "Well, that's another matter entirely. I'm sure we will need to have many hours rehearsing. Hazel can be my inspiration. And we mustn't forget the wombats with hairy noses."

***

Miss Atkins and Muriel staggered under a quantity of bags containing theatrical costumes, hats, props, and music sheets. Most of the public who had been chosen to perform in the reading afternoon were present and gathered in individual groups discussing their work or declaiming verses loudly to a disinterested assembly. Belinda, Hazel, and Charles entered the rehearsal room.

The black figure of Madam Perrot was rehearsing two effete late teenage males. "Now then," said Madam in a voice riddled with confidence, I am reinstating 'the Gribsby episode,' deleted by Oscar Wilde, which involves the arrival of a solicitor to arrest Algernon, who is posing as the fictitious Ernest, for unpaid bills. I have made specific alterations to the text. We will do the scene again, this time with less sibilance and more machismo. I will read Jack's lines again. Commence!"

The taller of the two men spoke, "Mister Ernest Worthing?"

His chubby associate replied, "Yes."

"Of B Four, The Albany?

"Yes, that is my address."

"I am very sorry, Mister Worthing, but we have a writ of attachment for twenty days against you for a quantity of lace, seven hundred and sixty two pounds."

"What perfect nonsense!"

Madam took her cue. "Kindly allow me to see this bill, Mister Gribsby. I am bound to say I never saw such reckless extravagance in all my life. Seven hundred and sixty two pounds for lace! How grossly materialistic!"

Out of the corner of her eye, she saw Belinda and Hazel. "Keep rehearsing boys, and remember, machismo!" She lifted the skirt of her long, black lace-covered dress and made her way across the room. "I hope you've got your lines down, Miss Whitby, and I see you have brought along your Jack Worthing." Madam extended her hand to Charles, "How do you do, I'm Madam Malefic.

Belinda looked at Charles to gauge his reaction. He frowned, ran his eyes over the creature in black that stood before him. "Err...Madam?"

"Madam, may I introduce St Mathew's vicar in Abbey Combe, the reverend Charles Mead."

Madam Perrot acknowledged him with a faint nod and a curl of the lip, which she intended as a smile. She turned to Belinda. "It would be a great help if you could assist Miss Atkins and Muriel with the costumes and props. I doubt their ability. And Miss Whitby, please begin your rehearsal. You have your scripts?" Without waiting for a reply, she returned to the two youths.

"I've never seen that woman before," said Charles excitedly, "she's not the woman who introduced herself to me as Madam Malefic. Totally different woman."

"Thank you," said Belinda, "you've confirmed our suspicions. And she didn't recognise you either. I'll explain it all later."

Hazel took his arm and led him to a quiet corner of the room. "I don't understand," said Charles, "what's going on?"

"Murder," said Hazel, "but let's get this bloody rehearsal out of the way and we can explain everything."

Belinda joined Muriel and began to sort through bags of costumes.

Hazel glanced at her script. "Found?" She sat down on a worn chaise longue. "Found?" she sneered, dropping character. "Don't pull my leg –"

Charles, still bewildered from meeting the substitute Madam Malefic, dropped his script in exasperation. "Stop ad libbing."

Hazel selected an anachronistic nineteen-twenties Cloche hat, which was to be an indication of her future costume. "Shut up and let's get on with it. I'm getting a chill.'

Charles scowled at her, lifted his script, and read, "The late Mr Thomas Cardew, an old gentleman, etc., etc., etc., found me and gave me the name of Worthing, etc., etc. etc., It is a seaside resort."

Hazel tried to hide a yawn but failed, giving Charles a fairly substantial view of the passage to her larynx. "And where did this bloke find you?" she slurred.

"In a handbag."

Hazel knew that somehow she had to take the curse off her next line. "Edith Evans owns that, and everyone's tried to force it out of her steely grasp. Business? A bit of business?" She looked around and called to Belinda. "Can you bring me a bag of some sort?"

Belinda sorted through the props and selected a large paper carrier bag, which bore the name of a fashionable Bond Street boutique. "Will this do?" She handed it the Hazel, who inspected it.

"It'll do. I want her to speculate on the possibility of a baby fitting into her handbag. "Found?" she muttered as she proceeded to open the bag. But what met her eye caused her to freeze.

A large carving knife.

Covered in dried blood.

"Shit," said Lady Bracknell.

Chapter Eleven

Belinda put down the phone. "That was the police." Hazel looked up from a recipe book. "Let me guess. The blood on the knife is from someone's Sunday roast, probably rare roast beef. I've just read a green salsa recipe that would go well with it."

"The blood is human."

"Oh," said Hazel taken aback, "that's a different keddle of fish."

"What's more," said Belinda as she poured a cup of tea, "they've tested the blood, and it doesn't match the body found in the garden." Hazel was silent as she absorbed this new information. "I don't have to tell you what that means. Another murder."

"You don't know that," said Hazel, "maybe someone cut their hand."

Belinda shook her head. "No. This wasn't just an accident. Forensics say the blood came from an artery, and it's from a female."

"Hang on, if it's not from the real Madam Malefic buried in the garden, then who is this?"

Belinda took a sip of tea before replying. "Given that the knife was found in a bag belonging to Miss Atkins and Muriel, I think they may have to answer a few questions."

"But the police will have done that, surely?"

"True. But I can ask questions the police can't."

***

Abbey Almshouses consisted of twenty bedroom units built "For Ten Poor Men and Ten Poor Women of the Parish. Eighteen forty-five," said Belinda reading the foundation stone. In the shadow of St Mathew's, the structure held the worst of Victorian architectural revival style. There was no response when Hazel knocked on the wooden door of what the caretaker with inquisitive eyes had assured them was Muriel Meldrew's residence.

"Been some strange comings and goings these days," he proffered in an enquiring tone. "Police. Never seen the like." But Belinda and Hazel thanked him, left him in his ignorance, and proceeded along the path to the main building. Disheartened at the prospect their visit was to be in vain, they turned to leave when Muriel stepped out of the communal laundry building, clutching a basket of fresh washing. She scowled as she made her way towards them. "Go away. I have nothing to say to you."

"We wanted to know how the knife got into the bag you brought to the rehearsal," said Belinda.

"I've told the police all I know," said Muriel frostily as she unlocked the door. "I don't have to tell you anything."

"The police say you're a witness to a crime," said Hazel.

Muriel turned quickly. "The police said that?"

Hazel looked sheepish. "Well, no. I was just —"

"Just what?" demanded Muriel angrily. "There's such a thing as defamation, and if you go around the village telling lies about me...well I..."

"Sorry, Muriel," said Belinda to placate the woman at the same time giving Hazel a disapproving look, "we aren't doing that, and we haven't spoken to the police, at least not about you, but it does seem odd that, what is now known to be a murder weapon, was in your possession."

Muriel shook her head. "No, it wasn't. It was in a bunch of bags and charity clothing that was left at the vicarage. We just picked them up when Madam wanted costumes and props for the rehearsals."

"Where is Madam now?" said Hazel.

Muriel glared at her. "I'm not speaking to you." She turned to Belinda. "Madam has taken Miss Atkins to London. The police questions upset her, and Madam felt she needed to get away for a while."

"And what about Darcy and the Captain?"

"The Captain drove them in the carriage. Darcy is still at Kryme Cottage. Now just go away and leave me alone."

The bang of the door slamming shut sent Belinda and Hazel on their way. As they left the houses, Belinda paused. "With Darcy left alone, now might be a good time to have a little chat with him. You chat with Charles, and I'll deal with Darcy."

Hazel turned to her. "Me? Talk to Charles?

What about?"

"Muriel said the bags came as part of charity items left at the vicarage. If that's true, how is it a murder weapon was included. Charles might have a few answers."

"Why don't you ask him. I'll talk to Darcy." Belinda looked at her friend with a questioning smile. "You'd scare him to death, and we'd learn nothing. No, you question Charles and leave Madam Perrot's little nephew to me."

Grumbling under her breath, Hazel set off for the vicarage, while Belinda made her way to Kryme Cottage. All was silent. Belinda wondered if she was on a wild goose chase. Darcy might not be in. But after a few raps on the door, she noticed the window shutters quiver a little. Convinced he was home and scrutinizing her, Belinda knocked again, loudly, and called, "Darcy? I know you're there. Open the door. I want to speak to you." Again there was silence.   As Belinda was about to knock once more, the door eased open, revealing a wary eye assessing her. Belinda pushed the door as it swung back to reveal Darcy in the act of shrinking away from her. Belinda recalled the night she had first set eyes on Darcy when Madam Perrot, unannounced and dripping with snow, had appeared on her doorstep. He seemed as flimsy as a shadow in her wake, and even now, as he stood before her, his lack of substance made Belinda want to reach out to touch him to confirm he was solid flesh and blood.

Making her way past Darcy, she entered the

main chamber. Boxes of household utensils and books lay scattered around, while an attempt had been made to make the inhospitable room more comfortable. "I'm told Madam is in London," said Belinda as Darcy followed her sheep-like.

"Yes. With Miss Atkins, who was taken poorly," replied Darcy timidly.

Belinda looked through a pile of books. They were all of Jane Austen's novels and writings. "Madam seems to have an interest in Jane," said Belinda, "she promised me a book of poems to read at the theatre, but never gave them to me." She looked up to the portrait of Jane Austen. "Why that interest, do you think? I know many people are devoted to her works, but...on the night of our séance, she wanted to talk to my aunt Jane's spirit but contacted a different Jane. Was it Jane Austen?" she turned a quizzical eye on him. "And she calls you Darcy. Is that your real name?"

The man looked away. "No," he said softly, "no. My real name is Joe. Joe Rankin."

"Is there a reason your aunt doesn't call you by your real name?"

Darcy glanced back at her. "She's not my aunt."

Belinda put down the Austen book she was holding. "If not your aunt, who is this Mrs Perrot?

Darcy reacted to the name. Avoiding Belinda's eye, he moved over to a collection of vinyl records and began to sift through them. "That's not her name."

Belinda moved to his side. "Really? I know it's not Malefic, but now you tell me it's not Perrot. What's the big mystery? She's not your aunt, so how is it you are working with her?"

"I'd rather not say."

"Nonsense, surely you can tell me that. It's not as though you have a criminal record or -" She stopped suddenly as Darcy cringed. "Oh, you do have a criminal record?"

Darcy turned away from her. "It was nothing really. An accident," he bleated, "I didn't know she couldn't swim, but they said I killed her. Drowned her." He turned to Belinda pleadingly, "I was only seven. She was three. I was taken from my parents and put into care until I was eighteen. They gave me a new name and released me. My parents were dead by then. Madam agreed to take me on as her secretary. She renamed me, Darcy."

Belinda was taken aback by this confession. "Oh, Darcy...Joe, I'm sorry to hear that. But I suppose Madam's actions in taking you in have been some benefit to you?"

Darcy looked at her in disbelief. "Are you out of your mind?"

Belinda took this spark of defiance as a sign that all was not well in his relationship with Madam Perrot. Taking her time to phrase her next question, she picked idly at the vinyl records, selecting one with no label and a whitish colour with streaks of grey and black. Distracted by this unusual disc, she said, "This is strange. Do you know what it is?"

Darcy gave a slight moan and snatched the record from her hands. "Don't touch that," he said in a voice filled with dread, "that's Madam's special recording. She plays it at séances to summon up the spirits." He slipped it into a paper sleeve and wiped his hands on his clothing as though he had been handling something dirty.

Belinda grinned. "We'll meet again, no doubt. But getting back to Madam, or Mrs Perrot, what does –"

Darcy cut her off. "Perrot is not her name," he said with a return of spirit.

"Good lord, how many names does she have?"

"Her real name is Entwhistle. Gladys Entwhistle."

Belinda laughed at the commonplace name bestowed on the woman. "And I bet she's not married, either?"

Again Darcy showed some daring, "Who would take that risk?"

Belinda began to warm to Darcy. Beneath the hangdog expression and aura of submission, she sensed a rebel. "And what are you required to do as Gladys's secretary?"

Darcy shrugged thin shoulders. "Just about anything she wants doing."

"So you would know why she wanted Kryme Cottage so badly. Badly enough to kill for it."

The man looked away and turned his back on Belinda. "You'd better go. I don't know what you're talking about."

"I think you do," said Belinda as she fronted him.

Darcy looked at her with such frightened eyes she could see it was pointless to pursue the matter. "Do you have a pen and paper?"

Darcy moved to a table and gave her a pen and a note pad. Belinda took them and started to write. "This is my phone number. If you are in any trouble with madam, call me."

Darcy took the note and glanced at it. "What makes you think I'll be in trouble?"

"Female intuition," said Belinda as she turned and left. Darcy stood in silence, squinted at the note, and shivered.

Chapter Twelve

Hazel gratefully accepted the gin and tonic proffered by Charles. She had not been comfortable since arriving at the Vicarage, for her interrogation regarding the discovery of a murder weapon in items originating from there. But she had to admit that Charles was being the soul of discretion and kept his distance. "Tell me about this woman calling herself Madam Malefic," said Charles as he sat opposite her, "and what happened to the woman who visited me using that name?"

"We believe she was found dead in Belinda's garden," said Hazel, thinking it was an excellent gin for a Vicar to select, "and we believe the woman calling herself Madam, killed her."

"Sin," said Charles softly.

"Pardon?"

"Sorry," said Charles with a dry smile, "Sin. It's all around us."

"If you say so," said Hazel taking a slug of gin. She hoped he wasn't about to launch into ecclesiastical by-laws and matters of immorality. Of course, she realised that murder would qualify as a basis for such debates, but now she just wanted to stick to her agenda. The murder weapon. "What's bothering us is the bloodstained knife found in items, which apparently came from here, the vicarage."

"A murder weapon? Yes, that's a bit of a mystery. According to Heckle and Jeckle, it was in a bag that was given with charity items. That's possible, as I don't really have much to do with that side of things. But there is no evidence to prove that it was."

"So someone could have slipped it in at any time?"

"Someone like me?" asked Charles with a questioning smile.

Hazel took another sip of gin to calm herself. He really did have a wonderful smile. "Well, there are some questions concerning you that, if answered, might clear up matters."

"Such as?"

"We've seen you entering Kryme Cottage."

Charles sank back into his chair. "Really? Seen me? Have you been spying on me."

Hazel felt she was entering deep waters. What if he had killed the real Madam Malefic? Would he hesitate to kill again? "Not spying really. It was an accident."

"How can you accidentally see me?"

"It was on a drone." Hazel explained how Quentin had seen him while using it.

"And you have a video of this?" said Charles. Hazel nodded. "Well, in that case, there is no use me denying it. Yes, I have been to Kryme Cottage, but never to see either version of Madam. When I first knew I was coming here, to Abbey Combe, I researched the area and stumbled across some information that interested me, the cottage in particular. I tried to purchase it, but failed, and then the real Madam bought it."

Hazel frowned. "But why would you want to buy Kryme Cottage?"

Charles rose to refill Hazel's glass. "Put it down to a whim. So your interrogation is, I imagine, because I am suspected of being a murderer, that the knife came from here at the vicarage, and I was careless in disposing of it. But you already claim the real Madam was killed by the fake Madam and dumped in Belinda's garden. So who am I guilty of murdering?" He leaned close and smiled as he handed Hazel the gin. She accepted it gratefully and wasted no time in sampling it. The interview was not going as she had expected. "The missing reverend Lamb?" she said in a half-whisper.

Charles gave a hoot of laughter and refreshed his own drink. "You are assuming the missing reverend has been murdered. Missing in action is more like it. And please don't think I'd bump off a teammate for the enviable pleasure of life in Abbey Combe." He ran his eyes over Hazel. "Of course, pastoral life here could be so much more pleasant if one was to have a convivial partner." To her horror, Hazel felt herself blush! Taking note of the rosy bloom, Charles continued, "I'm free tomorrow for lunch. Will you join me over at Norton Saint Phillip? The George hotel's home cooked honey glazed ham is heavenly."

***

"Gladys Entwhistle," said Belinda as she peeled potatoes, "our fake Madam Perrot's name is really Gladys Entwhistle. Would you believe?" Hazel unbuttoned her coat and leaned against the kitchen bench. "How do you know?"

"Darcy. Or should I say Joe, told me."

"This is getting confusing. Darcy. Joe? Gladys? I thought Madam Perrot's name was Mrs Perrot?"

"Apparently not," said Belinda splashing oil and herbs on the potatoes and placing them in the oven. "But I do admit that's confusing."

"Darcy offered no explanation?"

"No. It's obvious Gladys, or Madam Perrot, has a history of intrigue with all these false names, but it doesn't explain why she would murder the real Madam Malefic to get access to the cottage. What's there that is so important to her?"

"Search me," said Hazel, reaching for the coffee grinder, "and after talking to Charles, I still don't know why he's interested as well." There was a short pause as they waited for the coffee grinder to complete its noisy task. "He claims no knowledge of the knife and never met the fake Madam Perrot until the theatre rehearsal, but admits to secretly visiting the cottage. He has a key and visits when he suspects the owner is not at home."

Belinda inhaled the coffee aroma. "You told him we saw him on the drone?"

Hazel nodded. "I felt I had to, to convince him that we knew he was up to something. But got no further than his admission, he had wanted the cottage."

"He and Madam Perrot both wanted the cottage. But why?"

Hazel gave an imitation of being coy. "Charles wants to have lunch with me."

"That's good. Gives you another chance to find out more about him."

Hazel looked bothered. "Why don't you go? You know you fancy him. He might reveal more to you."

Belinda thought. Yes, she did find him attractive but was realising his predilection was for Hazel. "I think it's pretty clear he has you in his sights. Just go to lunch with him. It's not as though he's going to stick a knife into you. At least not in a public place," she added impishly.

***

It was the first of April, and Quentin felt himself to be the April Fool. He was deeply attracted to Belinda, but it seems that she didn't reciprocate. Over the past few weeks, while he'd been absent from Milford, it had given him a chance to review the situation and plan for his return. It was very early in the morning as he made his way into Richmond Park. He chose to walk, camera at the ready, to capture roaming deer, all lit by the rising sun's misty glow. He'd have to return in a few weeks to catch the floral display of Isabella Plantation in its woodland garden when it would be in full bloom. The Azaleas, Rhododendrons, Camellias, plus many other rare and unusual trees and shrubs would provide a dazzling display of colour to counter the more severe photos he'd taken of London for the tourist magazine.

As the mist began to lift, he drew the drone from his camera case and prepared it for flight. Some high shots of the magnificent park would accompany the land-bound ones. Setting it in flight, he watched the panorama spread out on the video feed via the drone's controller screen. It swooped down across treetops and then up, up to reveal the full glory of the park. He moved the controls bringing the drone over to the Pen Ponds, the mid-eighteenth century lake, divided in two by a causeway. The various trees gave a totally refreshing look to the already lush surrounding. Deer wandered freely around the area.

As attractive as the image on the video screen was, Quentin felt his mind slip back to thoughts of Belinda. They really hadn't had a chance to be together and get to know each other, and that harridan, Hazel, was clouding the issue. He would have to make it clear to her he wasn't interested. So, lost in his thoughts, it was with some surprise he saw a familiar object on the video screen. He directed the drone a little lower. "It's a Phaeton!"

He watched the horse-drawn carriage make its way beneath the trees then out into the open space by the Ponds. Some bird life disturbed the calm surface of the water as the carriage drew to a halt. A female figure in black emerged and turned back to the carriage to drag a woman out. The woman struggled and fell to the ground.

A sudden roar nearby drew Quentin's attention to a large Stag, which looked distinctly unhappy to meet a human while on his morning stroll. Swiftly, Quentin returned the drone to the home base and set off in the direction of the Ponds. It was some distance and some time before he reached the water's edge.

But all was quiet.

Madam Malefic, the woman, and the Phaeton had gone.

In the far distance, a few joggers and walkers made their appearance. Quentin withdrew into the shade of the trees. He sat on his haunches, and as he began to remove the drone from his case, was aware of a sound behind him and half turned as a dark shape descended on him.

He heard the crunch of bone before he toppled over and blacked out, unaware of the blood streaming from his head.

Chapter Thirteen

Charles slipped the key into Kryme Cottage's door. He congratulated himself on having the foresight to copy the key, after convincing the agent he was considering buying the property.

It was still early morning, and all was quiet. The villagers were at their breakfast, and the streets and paths were empty. The sun struggled to break through the network of branches in the tangle of trees hiding the cottage but failed, condemning the building to be forever in shade.

Charles closed the door behind him. Softly. He knew Madam Perrot was in London if he was to believe the information relayed by the surly Muriel, who curiously seemed almost unwilling to discuss anything relating to the cottage or about the false Madam, who Hazel claims is a murderess. He could hear a rustling sound and crept cautiously across the entrance hall into the main room. The space was almost as dark as midnight with no sunlight, but he could make out a figure standing at a table. The figure, muttering to itself, seemed intent on some obscure activity, suddenly became aware of his presence and turned. Charles could make out the pale features of Darcy.

"Switch on a light," he ordered in a voice of authority. Darcy moved slowly to a lamp and turned it on. He was revealed in his pyjamas and stared at Charles as though he had seen a ghost.

"Sorry to startle you," said Charles advancing further into the room, "I was given to understand the cottage was empty."

Darcy began to breathe a little easier. "Madam is in London." He glanced at the table. Charles followed the glance. A book was half wrapped in brown paper. Charles picked it up. "Jane Austen, her Times," he read aloud. "A fan of Austen, are you?"

Darcy shook his head. "Madam is."

Charles glanced around at the Austen portrait. "And what is it your Madam finds so appealing. Her writing? Her times? Her personality? Her secrets?

"Secrets," said Darcy softly, as though shame-facedly admitting to a sin during confession.

Charles raised an eyebrow. "Madam seems surrounded by secrets, doesn't she? What particular skeleton in Austen's cupboard does she find so appealing? A secret lover, for example?"

Again Darcy shook his head.

"Not a lover? How disappointing. I always find it encouraging when we discover the gods have feet of clay. So, if not love, what?"

Darcy fumbled nervously with his pyjama cord. "I don't really understand. But it has something to do with...lace."

"Lace? What sort of lace?"

Darcy cowered a little. "Please, I don't know. I shouldn't have told you. Now you'd better go. Madam will be back soon, and I don't think she'd like to find you here or know I'd been talking to you."

"I'm sure she wouldn't," said Charles, "and probably best not to tell her. I don't think she'd welcome my interest in the cottage." He turned and left, ruminating on the curious discovery that Madam Perrot was fixated on lace, which would explain in part why she wore so much of it.

Darcy waited for a moment to ensure he was alone before scrawling something on the book's flyleaf and wrapping it in the brown paper covering. The thunderous sound of a horse and carriage careering along nearby roads caused him to look up in alarm. Hurriedly, he grasped the packaged book, switched off the light, and clambered up the rickety staircase to his room.

Outside, Charles heard the approaching carriage and took shelter among the foliage. He watched as the Phaeton drew to a halt outside the cottage, and the woman in black descended. She gave some curt instructions to Captain, who was the driver, then walked to the front door. Captain slapped the reins setting the horses to their burdensome task of transporting their master to the stables.

Inside, Madam entered the main room and paused. Something was different. She sensed an unwelcome presence.

All was still.

Everything was quiet.

She sniffed. There was a strange scent. Someone, a stranger, had been in the cottage. She glanced upwards. Darcy must still be in bed. With firm steps, she approached the staircase.

***

Quentin was amazed at how easy it was to fly. He was looking down on London and could see the changing of the guard at Buckingham Palace, but the soldiers were not in their regular uniforms. Some wore green, others pink. And then he was flying over water, water, water, until he was unexpectedly moving slowly along the Champs Elysée. Other people were walking, but he was floating just a few feet off the ground. With a whoosh, he shot upwards into an intense blue sky. He heard voices, some far off, others close by. He tried to understand what they were saying. He heard snippets. "traumatic" "emergency" "relieve pressure". The bright blue sky began to darken as though a storm was approaching. With a roar, the darkness descended, abruptly sealing off all sight and sound.

"Immediate CT without delay. The usual procedure," said the doctor as he left the emergency ward.

***

Mona had finished her work for the day and returned home. Hazel was on her way to lunch with Charles at Norton St Phillip, so for the first time in many weeks, Belinda was alone in the cottage. She was restless and felt the need for company. Quentin hadn't returned from his work in London, and his phone didn't respond to any of her calls. She assumed that he might be working somewhere out of range, but it did seem odd. A glance in the refrigerator for something to quell hunger pains revealed a container of leftover Beef Bourguignon, which had turned an interesting shade of green. Having grown used to Hazel's newly discovered cooking skills, she felt reluctant to prepare lunch for herself and decided to try the new menu at the Ship & Anchor pub. Shrugging on a warm coat, she made her way down the hill and past her famous garden.

The warmth of a blazing fire greeted her as she stepped into the old building. There were a few villagers in the dining room, and at the bar, she saw two tradesmen, their overalls smeared with the colourful remnants of paint secured from numerous renovations. The barman hailed her. "Belinda, lass. What takes your fancy?"

"A pint please, Oliver, and I'll have lunch when a table is free." She watched as he pulled a pint, his rotund figure squeezed in behind the bar. Oliver, she knew, had been 'something in the city', had taken early retirement to become a landlord in a setting vastly different from his life in the City. He placed the beer on the bar and waddled off in the direction of the dining room. Belinda took a sip of beer and relaxed against the bar. She became conscious she was being watched, and glancing to her side saw one of the painters smiling at her and recognised him as the man climbing the ladder to replace roof tiles on Kryme Cottage.

"G' day. Cold enough for you?"

Belinda was startled to hear an Australian accent. "Good grief," she said with a smile, "what are you doing so far from home?"

The painter smiled broadly. "I knew it was you. I'd heard there was an Aussie living in the village. I'm just on a working holiday. 'names Jack, by the way, and this is Tom. He's a Pom. But he's alright, really. The two men jovially nudged each other.

Belinda shook hands with them. "I'm Belinda, from Melbourne. You?"

"Brisbane," said Jack. "Can't wait to get back to some sunshine."

"You did some work on Kryme Cottage?"

Jack and Tom exchanged an amused glance. "Too right," said Jack, "I've had some odd jobs, but that was weird."

"In what way," said Belinda taking a sip of beer.

"Well, that old duck for a start, Madam Malefic. I won't tell you what we called her behind her back. She seemed to be looking for something." He turned to Tom, "Remember how she smashed up that cupboard.

Tom nodded, "Made a right mess of it."

"There was this small wooden cupboard with a lock like a devil's face," continued Jack, "and she seemed desperate to find a key to unlock it. She tried, must have been about twenty keys, but had no luck, so in desperation, she smashed it open with a hammer."

"What did she find?" said Belinda.

"Nothing. It was empty. That really pissed her off. Ranted and raved about the place like a looney. From then on, she told us to keep an eye out for any signs the walls had been tampered with. She was forever searching with a torch, looking for cracks that might show if there was a hidden recess anywhere."

"Did she find anything?"

Jack shook his head. "Nah. Not a thing. If you ask me, I think she's a screw loose. We were pretty pleased when she paid us and we were shot of Kryme Cottage."

They were joined by an elderly man who made his way from the dining room. "Did you say Kryme Cottage? Nasty place, nasty."

Belinda turned to him. "Why do you say that?"

"It's haunted," said the man, indicating to Oliver behind the bar that he wanted another pint.

Jack and Tom gave snorts of derision. "Oh, you can scoff," said the man, "but those of us here know only too well its history."

"I've heard tell of a woman in black, who appeared at night by horse and carriage," said Belinda.

The man took a sip of his fresh, pulled pint. "You've heard that have you? Lots say it's just a pile of nonsense, but my family's been living in Milford for seven generations, and we have letters written from times past saying it did happen. She'd stay at Kryme Cottage, then disappear, always at night. And she always wore black."

"Do the letters say when this happened," said Belinda.

"Can't recall offhand, but some of them date back to the eighteenth century and Georgian times in Bath. Could be when that happened, lots of fashionable ladies and gents from London bought houses hereabouts." He took another slurp of beer and nudged Belinda. "To be near the shenanigans going on at the roman baths," he added with a wink.

After a filling lunch of sausages and mash, Belinda made her way back up the hill. Her mind was stewing over the recent discussion on the mysterious lady in black who had visited Kryme Cottage all those years ago. Who was she, and why had she been so secretive? And why did Madam Perrot seem to imitate her?

A sharp shower of icy rain made her scurry for cover at her front door where a small parcel, wrapped in brown paper, was beginning to soften beneath the moisture. Entering the hall, she shook the rain from her coat, shivered, made her way to the long room to stir the fire embers into life. Throwing on a fresh log, she tore open the parcel. It was an old book, well-worn, with an unremitting, dank smell that indicated mildew. "Probably the book of poems Madam Perrot had promised to send," she muttered to herself. Opening it she read the title,

JANE AUSTEN Her Times. She wouldn't bother with it now, as she wondered if the Theatre Royal event would now take place. She dropped the book on the sofa and, settling in a chair by the fire, turned on the television. Hazel would be back soon, and no doubt be full of minutiae about her lunch with Charles.

The early afternoon news programme was illustrating the usual grievances the world was suffering from. Belinda reached for the television guide. The last news item slipped by, only half-heard '...the discovery of a woman's body in the Pen Ponds at Richmond Park. The woman had been disfigured before being drowned, making identification difficult. The police are in attendance.'

Belinda switched the channel to a documentary on Hairy Nosed Wombats. The beer, sausages and mash, combined with comforting warmth, lulled her into a doze, so she was startled when Hazel shook her by the shoulder, "Wake up. Any news?"

Belinda yawned, "I was rather hoping you had some."

Hazel threw off her coat and sat on the sofa. "I don't know what you mean," she said bashfully.

"Give over, what happened with Charles?"

"Do you know, he was really quite charming. Didn't get touchy feely and talked about his family and growing up, that sort of thing."

"And?"

"Oh, he wanted to know all about me and what I'd done with my life".

Belinda smiled. "I hope you gave him the expurgated version."

Hazel looked offended. "Well, if you're going to be like that!"

"Sorry, I was just teasing," said Belinda, still with a smile.

Hazel looked about as though to change the subject. She saw the Jane Austen book and opened it. "What's this?"

Belinda glanced at her. "Oh, it was on the doorstep. I guess it's from Madam Perrot. The poetry reading and all that."

Hazel frowned. "But this inscription on the flyleaf? What does it mean? 'Look at page one hundred and twenty six'?"

Belinda sat up. "Hand it over." She took the proffered book and read the inscription before turning to the page indicated.

"What does it say?" said Hazel eagerly.

"She denied stealing the lace," read Belinda, "believing the salesclerk made a mistake but was still arrested on a charge of grand theft. The lace she was believed to have stolen was worth over twenty shillings and brought the death sentence. The accused was Jane Austen's mother's sister-in-law, Jane Leigh Perrot."

Chapter Fourteen

Hazel's eyes opened wide. "But... isn't that the –"
"- the name Madam Perrot gave when I saw her in the shop in Bath, yes," said Belinda, "that's what the shop girl told me, and she was looking for lace. Old lace."

Hazel sank back into the sofa. "This is getting crazy! Now she's claiming to be a woman who existed... how many years ago?"

"Over two hundred or so," muttered Belinda as she continued to read the book. "If this woman was Jane Austen's mother's sister-in-law, that would make her Austen's aunt by marriage." She put down the book and looked thoughtful. "Remember, at the seance, Madam Perrot claimed she was talking to someone called Jane? If it wasn't *my* Aunt Jane, maybe it was Jane Austen, and she wanted to talk to *her* aunt."

Hazel leapt to her feet. "I need a drink. This is getting too weird to be true."

Belinda was still lost in thought. "And she talked about lace, remember? White and black lace." She picked up the book. "Listen to this. Mrs Leigh-Perrot stopped off to procure some black lace. As she left, she was confronted by the proprietor. It was noticed that some valuable white lace was also in the package. Mrs Leigh-Perrot claimed a worker must have accidentally put the white lace in with the black. A few days later, she was detained for shoplifting and jailed."

"All well and good," said Hazel, as she splashed a modicum of tonic water into her glass of gin, "but what's the connection with all that and Madam Perrot murdering Madam Malefic. Also, who left the book for you? And why?"

The phone rang, and Belinda answered it. Hazel took her drink and went to the kitchen to prepare coffee. As she switched off the grinder, she looked up to see Belinda standing in the doorway. "What's the matter with you? You're pale as a ghost."

"That was a London hospital. It's Quentin. He's in intensive care and not expected to live."

***

"I'm afraid we had to put him into a medically induced coma. Brain injuries, such as he has, often result in considerable swelling of the brain. That puts pressure on the brain and decreases blood flow and oxygen supply, damaging brain tissue. Inducing a coma allows the brain to rest," said Doctor Smyth. Belinda and Hazel stood with him as they watched through the intensive care window as a nurse attended to Quentin. He lay prone, a multitude of tubes and wires binding him to the hospital bed.

"How was he injured?" asked Hazel wiping tears from her eyes. Dr Smyth looked at her. Seeing she was upset, he took her arm. "Come with me, I'll explain what the police discovered. He led them through several corridors until they reached a small office. Belinda and Hazel followed the tall, grey-haired figure as he ushered them in and offered seats to them before he took his place at a desk. "What I know is, the police were alerted to a report of an injured man in Richmond Park. Some joggers discovered him and called the police. He had lost an amount of blood. The paramedic nurse treated him before bringing him here. It seems Mister de La Tour had been attacked and beaten with a solid piece of wood. He sustained, as I've already said, severe wounds to the head."

"Do the police have any idea who attacked him?" said Belinda.

"Not so far, I'm afraid. They're seeking witnesses."

"How did you know to contact me? Quentin is a neighbour, but we've only known each other for a few months."

"Police found a wallet in his jacket with a photograph of you, which had your name and phone number."

"A photo?" Belinda looked at Hazel. "When did he photograph me?"

Hazel shook her head and wiped her eyes. "Doctor. Does he have any family members that need to be contacted."

"The police have contacted his sister, who lives in Germany. We are keeping her abreast of his situation. We've also advised the travel company he was employed by on their photographic assignment."

"Do the police have his camera case and equipment?" said Belinda.

Dr Smyth shook his head. "The information we received from the police, he had nothing, or nothing was found, apart from the wallet I mentioned. As a professional photographer, he would have had a camera case, I imagine? I suppose that could have been the reason for the attack. Someone wanting the valuable equipment, but I'm sure the police would have considered that. My concern is to see that Mister de La Tour recovers and returns to full health."

***

Hazel was gloomy and quiet on the train journey back to Bath. Belinda knew of her friend's genuine fondness for Quentin, so to see him suffering and possibly dying had hit her hard. Both were silent as the train sped swiftly westwards, a journey Belinda recalled from all those years ago when she first visited Milford village, which led to her subsequent friendship with Hazel. Her thoughts returned to the present, and the doctor had left them with the parting words, 'only time will tell if the coma will work'. It was possible that Quentin's attacker was simply a thug who saw the value in the camera equipment and on the spur of the moment, in a lonely spot, took up a large piece of wood, struck him, and fled with the camera case, to sell off in some pub somewhere. The camera case might have also contained the drone. Was that a connection with the attack on Quentin? Something on the video it had recorded that someone wanted? Something that person wished to keep secret? There was Charles's video entering Kryme Cottage; he had admitted to that when Hazel spoke with him. But was there some reason he now wanted the video destroyed? Even Belinda herself found it difficult to believe that Charles would track down Quentin at dawn in Richmond Park and beat him senseless. Someone did. And Charles still held the secret of why he wanted Kryme Cottage.

***

Toast soldiers at the ready, Charles cracked open his boiled egg, sighed, and pushed it away. It was hard-boiled. Like a rock. Again. It had been ever since Muriel Meldrew took over preparing his meals while Miss Atkins was away in London. Last night's dinner was a travesty of cottage pie. How long this was to go on for was the question? He rose and made his way across the grounds to the Almshouses and knocked on Muriel's door. Muriel's greeting was brusque and frosty. Faced with this gorgon, Charles felt in need of Christian fortitude. He said, "'Morning, Muriel. Any news from Miss Atkins? Have you heard when she'll be returning?"

Muriel sniffed. "I don't know, I'm sure. It's one thing to claim you need a rest, another to wallow in self-pity. I believe she's still in London with Madam when she should be here helping with the brass and sorting out the flowers for next Sunday. You might have to put up with a dull lectern and just a few bits of green, so don't blame me."

In an attempt to soothe the woman, Charles assured her he would not apportion any blame. "But Madam returned from London yesterday," he continued, "I happened to be near Kryme Cottage and saw her arrive."

Muriel looked puzzled. "She's back? Was Atkins with her?"

"No, she was alone, except for the carriage driver, so I assume Miss Atkins is staying on in London and thought you might know when she plans to return."

Muriel was silent as she absorbed this news. "I...I don't understand it. Who would Atkins stay with in London? She has no family or none that I know of, and it's strange that Madam didn't contact me on her return. We had..." she broke off as though she feared she was thinking aloud.

"Well, thank you, Muriel. I think a visit to Madam is called for, just looking after one of my parishioners, you know, seeing after her welfare."

He turned and strode off in the direction of Kryme Cottage. Muriel watched him until he disappeared from sight, a worried frown on her brow, trembling hands matching the anxiety in her eyes.

As Charles approached the cottage, he was aware of heavy hammering from inside. His rap on the door sounded weak in comparison to the ringing sound of metal on metal, and he feared his knock would not be heard. But the door edged open, and amid a strong swell of peppermint, the bruised features of Darcy considered him.

"Darcy, is Madam in?" said Charles as he edged past the door and into the main room. He was startled to see Madam near a far window, hammer, and chisel in hand, chipping away at the wall. Nearby additional tools rested, a spade, a sledgehammer. There was evidence of additional defacement to the walls while a crack had appeared in the ceiling.

Madam was equally startled to find the vicar observing her. Hastily she dropped the tools, stepped over a small pile of rubble, and wiping her hands on her dress, approached him. "What do you want?" she asked, her voice querulous and breathless.

"I see you are doing alterations, Madam. What plans do you have?"

Madam glanced quickly at the broken stonework, "Oh...perhaps another lamp," she said without conviction.

Charles waited for her to continue, but she returned her gaze to him and stood erect her lady-of-the-manor persona returning.

"I was curious about Miss Atkins's health and wondering when she would return home?"

Madam tossed head and began to fiddle with a pile of books on the nearby table. She avoided looking at him. "Oh, Miss Atkins I fear is far from well. She has been admitted to a nursing home to gather her senses and recuperate. Time will tell when and if she is to return, but I suspect never."

"May I have the name of the nursing home, so I can contact her?"

Madam turned to him with a determined expression. "Reverend, I'm afraid I cannot do that. The doctors have assured me, the woman needs complete rest and is not to be reminded of recent events. The finding of that knife covered in blood, which so shocked her delicate emotions. She's not be reminded of anything relating to Abbey Combe or Milford. Please see yourself out. I have urgent business to attend to."

With this abrupt dismissal, Charles saw it was folly to pursue the matter, at least just then. He turned to find the bruised figure of Darcy opening the door, and as Charles stepped into the roadway, he once again, heard the hammer and chisel at work as Madam continued her secret undertaking.

***

Belinda toyed with a slice of toast. Her knife slowly spread butter from the centre to cover the piece from edge to edge, top to bottom. Strawberry jam followed the same pattern. This was done subconsciously as the mystery surrounding Madam Perrot, Quentin's attack, the missing vicar, and Charles' interest in Kryme Cottage combined to bustle around in her brain. They were all connected, and central to it all was the Cottage itself.

If she could only gain access to it without the presence of Madam Perrot, she might find clues that would help solve the problem. But how? Darcy's hesitant rebellion against his benefactor when last she spoke with him, suggested to Belinda she might have a potential collaborator in gaining access to an empty cottage, but just how he could help wasn't immediately apparent. She would discuss it with Hazel.

***

"Simple," said Hazel as she inspected her fingernails and thought over Belinda's problem, "you don't need Darcy's help. Charles has a key to the cottage, remember? Just ask him for it."

That wasn't the answer Belinda wanted. She was reluctant to tell Hazel of her caution regarding Charles; she still couldn't convince herself he was an innocent party. There was the Reverend Lamb, who conveniently went missing, permitting Charles to take up the ministry, plus his unexplained interest in the Cottage.

Getting the key was a good suggestion, but Belinda felt some diversion was required to allow her to access it. And Hazel was the perfect diversion. "No, I think a little subterfuge is called for. I don't want Charles to know my plans. We'll call on him this afternoon on some pretext. You can keep him busy while I steal the key. I think it is on the key rack inside the front door."

"How am I going to keep him busy," said Hazel disingenuously.

Belinda didn't bother to comment but continued. "If I can get the key, all we have to do is somehow arrange for Madam Perrot to be out of the cottage. And that's where Darcy can help us."

Chapter Fifteen

Charles greeted his afternoon guests with a hearty welcome. He had been preparing his Sunday sermon, 'consider the lilies of the field' and wondered how its objective of not worrying about worldly requirements would sit with his congregation, given that the few that sloped into church were either gentleman farmers, London bankers spending the weekend at their country cottage, or old-age pensioners who were constantly fretting if their pittance would last the month, so the unexpected diversion of time spent with Hazel, was manna from heaven.

Babbling a welcome, he took their coats and hung them on the hall stand. Belinda noted the key labelled 'k' was still hanging there. Initially she had thought it was labelled for the vicarage kitchen, but now was convinced the 'k' stood for Kryme Cottage.

Settled in the lounge, Charles began, "I'm glad you called. I have some news that might interest you. I've been told that Miss Atkins has –"

Belinda gave a sneeze and leapt to her feet. "Excuse me, I left my handkerchief in my coat pocket." Under Charles' suspicious gaze, she ran to the hall and swiftly took the 'k' key from the rack and put it deep in her coat pocket. Then tense with smugness, she resumed her place with the others. "Did you get it?" asked Charles.

Belinda looked bewildered for a moment. Did he mean the key? "Oh...you mean the handkerchief? Silly me, it was tucked in my sleeve all the time." As if to prove she wasn't lying, she removed it and ostentatiously wiped her nose.

Charles looked doubtful. "I've been telling Hazel that Miss Atkins has been committed to a nursing home and won't be returning here. What do you make of that?"

"How do you know?" said Belinda, feeling confident that she had got away with the theft.

"I called on Madam earlier and was told. It seems Miss Atkins took the discovery of the blood covered knife rather badly and had an attack of the vapours, which seems to be terminal."

The three discussed this development and the repercussions it would have on the village, church life, and Muriel Meldrew. "Does she know?" asked Belinda.

Charles shook his head. "I called on her after I left Kryme Cottage, but there was no answer. Whether she was home and didn't want to talk to me, I'm not sure, then I got busy with the damned sermon for Sunday."

Belinda rose. Suddenly feeling guilty and eager to get away, she said, "We'll call on Muriel and tell her the news. No doubt she will be upset." As Charles helped her on with her coat, he noticed the 'k' key was missing. His suspicions were confirmed. Belinda was up to something. It remained to be seen what.

Belinda could feel Charles's eyes burning into her back as they left the vicarage and made their way to the Almshouses.

It was some time before Muriel answered their knock, and reluctantly opened the door. Her eyes were red from weeping. A gentle wave of lavender filled the air as she placed an inefficient handkerchief to her nose. "What do you want."

"We have some bad news, I'm afraid," said Belinda. "We've just learned that Miss Atkins has been placed in a nursing home and won't be returning. As her friend, we thought you should know."

Muriel stared at them, her eyes opening wide. She gave a heartbreaking scream and covered her face with her hands, sobbing violently. Belinda, startled by this reaction, put her hand on the woman's arm to comfort her. Muriel shook it off and removed her hands to reveal a face racked with pain. "She's dead!" she shouted, "Do you understand? The woman is dead!" Her weeping increased, and she pulled away from them and slammed the door. They could hear her weeping and muttering to herself.

"Well," said Hazel, "I've heard of overreacting, but that's pure Oscar material."

"Don't be so insensitive," said Belinda, "but it was certainly dramatic, and why should she believe her friend to be dead?"

"Perhaps she always looks on the bleak side of life."

"Possibly, or maybe she regards being placed in a nursing home is as good as being dead?"

"Or she is actually dead."

Belinda looked at Hazel. "Meaning she regarded being taken to London and put in a home, as a metaphor for being murdered?"

Thinking about this, they began the walk back to Milford. They had just reached the corner near Quentin's cottage when they saw Darcy walking towards them, leading one of the horses that drew Madam Perrot's carriage. He paused, then continued on as though to ignore them. Hazel nudged Belinda, "Look at his cheek and eye." Belinda could see the bruises.

"Darcy, what on earth happened to your face?" said Belinda. Darcy shied away as he stopped and leaned against the horse. He touched his bruised cheek.

"Madam, she...that, I had a fall in the cottage. Those wooden stairs. They're old. Rickety. Dangerous, I keep telling madam." He looked at Belinda as though judging if she believed him. She didn't.

"You must be more careful, Darcy," she said meaningfully, "Madam should take better care of you. What are you doing with the horse?"

"Just having her reshod. Has to be done every month or so. Ready for a trip to Bristol."

"Oh, Bristol," said Belinda with false bonhomie, "I remember walking across Brunel's suspension bridge over the Avon Gorge. Not for the faint hearted. Cycling across at night is also a real treat. You should try it, Hazel."

Hazel rolled her eyes. "I've better night-time treats in mind, thank you."

Belinda turned to Darcy. "When is the trip?"

"Tomorrow. We leave early"

"A day trip?"

Darcy shook his head. "No, I think for a few days."

Belinda smiled to herself. "Well, I'm sure you will appreciate the break. Enjoy yourself." She and Hazel continued on to her cottage. Darcy stood watching them. The horse, eager to be away, shook her head and tugged at the rein. In deep thought, Darcy took a packet of peppermints from his pocket, popped one in his mouth, and then resumed his return to Kryme Cottage.

Belinda could not believe her luck. Fate was playing into her hands, and tomorrow she would have free access to Kryme Cottage. What she expected to find there she was unsure of but hoped to find some evidence that Madam Perrot was guilty of murdering Madam Malefic, and a reason why she was so determined to have the cottage even to the extent of killing to gain it.

***

The next day found Belinda on tenterhooks. She woke early, the morning stretching endlessly ahead of her. Her thoughts overnight had formed a belief as to why Madam Perrot was so determined to own Kryme Cottage, and she was keen to see if the visit there would confirm her suspicions. Darcy had said they would leave early, but how early? Dawn? Eight o'clock? Ten?

Hazel had suggested they should consider noon to be a safe time to deem Madam Perrot had departed, besides, she had no intention of rising before ten herself, so Belinda was forced to concoct things to keep herself occupied until the appointed hour. These consisted of making several cups of coffee, vacuuming the hall carpet, making a list of jobs for Mona to do next week, some half-hearted stretching exercises, and another three cups of coffee. Remembering how dark it had been on her previous visits to Kryme, she tucked a torch into her coat pocket. The sun was well and truly up but hadn't the power to break through Milford's heavy cloud.

Promptly at noon, hyped up on caffeine, she and Hazel set forth. It seems strange to be passing Quentin's deserted cottage, and Belinda reminded herself to ring the hospital when they returned to check on his recovery.

The path to Kryme Cottage was damp from recent rain, and still unsure if Madam Perrot had actually left, they slowed their walk to a snail's pace. When they arrived all was quiet, but they waited in the shadows of the trees for fully five minutes. Finally, Belinda could wait no longer and inhaling a deep breath, she led the way across the garden to the front door. She knocked. If anyone answered, she would make some excuse, but all was silent. With cold fingers, she fumbled with the lock, dropped the key, muttered some rich swear words, picked it up, and eventually succeeded in turning the key. As the door opened, it revealed the dank, dark interior, which would have deterred a less motivated interloper.

Belinda switched on the torch, the beam splitting the darkness to reveal a room in shambles. Furniture had been moved, books scattered the floor, and here and there, small piles of rubble lay beneath cracked walls.

"What are we looking for?" said Hazel.

"My instinct is for lace. Black and white lace," muttered Belinda as they moved into the centre of the room.

Hazel was distracted by the pile of vinyl records. She skimmed through them, peering at the labels. "Hmmm...Jane Austen novels. Audiobooks. "Sense and Sensibility, Pride and Prejudice." She picked up a white record. "What's this? There's no label."

Belinda glanced at it. "Oh, something she uses in her seances."

Hazel dropped the record, and they moved into the centre of the room. "Looking for lace? Why?" queried Hazel as she stumbled over some of the rubble.

"Just my guess," said Belinda. "We know she's obsessed with lace and Jane's aunt, Mrs Leigh Perrot. I believe she thinks Leigh Perrot used to live here, or at least come here to stay. Remember the village folktale of the woman in black who would arrive in a horse drawn carriage, stay a few days and then depart? No one ever saw her. I believe Madam Perrot thinks she is Mrs Leigh Perrot and is set on finding the stolen lace, which she believes is hidden here."

Hazel gave a nod of agreement. "You could be right. She's nuttier than any fruit cake Escoffier ever baked."

"And judging by the state of the walls, she thinks the lace is somewhere in the cottage and is determined to find it."

They proceeded toward the rear of the room and the old wooden staircase. "Let's look upstairs," said Belinda.

"Careful. Remember what Darcy said," Hazel muttered. Belinda, who didn't believe Darcy's story of a fall, put her foot on the bottom step, but it fell away beneath the pressure. The next step was too high for her to move up to. She swung the torch behind the steps. "Hazel, see that box. Pull it out, and I'll use it as a step."

Hazel reached down and pulled the heavy box into the torchlight's beam. They both stared at it.

"It's a camera case!" said Hazel in disbelief.

"What's more, it's Quentin's camera case. I'd know it anywhere," cried Belinda

"How did it get here," said Hazel as she bent to raise the unlocked lid. The torchlight lit up the inside of the case, revealing Quentin's cameras and equipment. And nestled in with them – his drone

Chapter Sixteen

"Did you find what you were looking for? And I'll have my key back, please." Charles put out his hand. Belinda blushed. "You knew I took it?"

Charles grinned. "I don't miss much. What's that you have?"

Belinda placed the camera case on the floor and opened it. "We found Quentin's camera and the drone. It's possible that he shot something or filmed something on the drone that might indicate what happened to him."

Charles lifted out the drone. "Do you know how they work?" asked Hazel. He gave her his alpha male smile. "No, but that won't stop me." He lifted a book of instructions from the case. "All I have to do is follow the directions."

Belinda impatiently paced the floor for the next interminable thirty minutes while Charles read the instructions and fiddled with the drone. Hazel sat in the lounge eyeing the array of bottles in the bar. It was well over the yardarm, and the tension had increased her requirements for a relaxing tipple.

Finally, Charles got to his feet. "Right! Follow me."

He led them to his study and switched on his computer. "The drone records the images on this SD card." He held up a small black object. "If I insert it into my computer, here," he slid the card into the

SD slot, "we should be able to see what Quentin recorded."

The three of them huddled around the computer screen as images began to flow. Firstly some images of Richmond Bridge as the drone steadily drifted above it. Then floating over the river towards Ham House. Finally, the picture of Richmond park at treetop level. Higher and higher until in the distance, Pen Ponds. The three viewers gave a gasp. "It's a Phaeton!" cried Belinda.

They watched as the carriage made its way to the Ponds and halted. A figure in black appeared and turned to drag a struggling woman out. Belinda's eyes were wide open. The woman tumbled to the ground. "It's Madam Perrot and Miss Atkins." The screen went black.

***

Belinda notified the police of the drone find, and as a result, an arrest warrant was issued for Madam Perrot, Darcy, and Captain Frederick. They informed Belinda and Hazel that the body found in Pen Ponds was that of Miss Atkins, and they believed the attack on Quentin had been made by, presumably, Captain Frederick, who then took the camera case and had hidden it in Kryme Cottage. A police watch had been placed on the cottage, and a search was underway in Bristol and surrounds.

The weeks passed, and early summer sun

had gently warmed the stone cottages of Milford. Quentin recovered but suffered memory loss and had been taken to Germany by his sister to undergo special treatment. Belinda's garden was in full bloom and the coach parties had returned, with garden lovers from all over the world, eager to take in the wonder of Capability Brown's vision, planned so many years ago.

There had been no sighting of Madam Perrot, so the police guard on Kryme Cottage was ended, with just the remnants of police tape, and a sealed locked door to remind the locals that there was still a murderer on the loose.

One bright and breezy morning, Hazel came down the stairs to find Mona putting on her sun hat before leaving after completing her household duties. She rummaged in her handbag and placed a book on the hall stand. Hazel picked it up. She read the title, "Lady Don't Fall Backwards, I've been looking for this for months. Where did you find it?"

"Oh," said Mona, indifferently, while touching up her lipstick, "I took it with me to read when I stayed with my daughter in Bristol. Forgot about it."

"Thank you very much," said Hazel, tartly, "you could have told me."

"Sorry, I'm sure," muttered Mona as she left, shutting the door firmly behind her.

Also muttering to herself, Hazel went into the long room, reclined on the sofa and started to read the book, searching through to a point where she remembered what had happened in the plot.

Belinda was at her computer writing an email to her parents, filling them in on the local gossip, and an update on the search for Madam Perrot. Suddenly the air was filled with a wild shriek from the long room. Startled, Belinda committed the sin of two typos.

Hazel came rushing in. "Bel! Listen. He, is a she!"

Belinda, used to Hazel's eccentricities, waited for a more lucid proclamation.

"Don't you see," Hazel continued excitedly, "we've been looking at it all wrong. We took the reverend Lamb to be a man, whereas he might be a woman. I mean, the vicar might have been a woman, and she is the one who was buried in your garden."

Belinda turned to her. "Where did you get that idea?"

Hazel waved the book at her. "It's in here. The police made that mistake in this story until the detective discovered the truth."

"If that's the case, where is Madam Malefic's corpse?"

"That's another issue," said Hazel, not to be put off her contention. "If it is the female vicar, it might be easier to prove. She came from Durham. There must be records of her up there that would identify the body."

"True," said Belinda as she considered this new development. "Charles never mentioned the vicar's sex, indeed why would he? But I'll ring him and ask."

Before she could dial the number, Hazel said, "He's away in Exeter all week at a church conference, won't be back until the weekend. He told me he was switching off his phone, as it is some sort of religious retreat, and they cut themselves off from the world and any distraction."

Convenient, thought Belinda. "In that case, we can call on Muriel. She's bound to know."

***

They discovered Muriel Meldrew tending a recently inhabited grave in the cemetery adjacent to the church. Belinda and Hazel, and most of the local villagers, had attended the funeral when the police released Miss Atkins' body for burial. It had been a solemn occasion, as the manner in which the deceased had met her maker was uppermost in everyone's mind. The solemnity was only spoiled when Hazel, scattering earth on the coffin, dropped her mobile phone into the grave. Much confusion reigned while funeral directors and graveyard staff made various half-hearted attempts to regain it, but success was only achieved when a lad from the village jumped into the open grave, scooped it up, and clambering out, handed it to Hazel, who's thanks she offered later that night at the Ship & Anchor.

The solemnity of that occasion was now replaced with melancholy as Muriel knelt and planted a rosemary bush at the foot of the grave. The irrational thought crossed Belinda's mind that the plant would not survive, being in the open and exposed to winter rains and snow. But if it eased Muriel's grief, so much the better. The woman seemed to ignore their presence as they stood by her.

"Muriel," said Belinda, "would you answer a question for us?"

Muriel dabbed at her eyes with a handkerchief, and again, the lavender old-world fragrance, infused the air. She turned teary eyes to them but remained silent.

"About the reverend Lamb?"

Muriel was suddenly alert and on guard. "What about Lamb?"

"Can you tell us if the reverend Lamb was a man or a woman?"

Muriel stood erect. "What is it to do with you?" she said harshly.

"Well, we assumed he was a man, but it has been suggested it was really a woman vicar, that being the way of things nowadays."

"And we suspect she has been murdered," added Hazel.

Muriel stepped back, sank down on a grave, put her face in her hands, and began to wail. Belinda and Hazel looked on in surprise. The wailing stopped, and Muriel began to speak, almost in a chant, a mixture of religious quotations, prayers, and what amounted to a confession.

"Our Father, who art...sorry, so sorry...it was her...evil woman...spawn of Satan...she knew...she forced us...kill...kill...the woman...take the cottage... knew our secret...new vicar...woman...not man... must be a man...do not permit a woman to teach or to have authority over a man...women should remain silent in the churches...the head of the woman is man... be submissive...guilty...guilty."

The rambling went on until it gradually faded out. Muriel raised a face now devoid of any spirit or energy. Belinda sat by her and held her hand. "Muriel, it's alright now to tell the truth, to tell what happened. You owe that to your friend, Miss Atkins."

Muriel studded her for a moment, as though measuring her worth to receive her confession, then sighed. "It was a woman vicar, you see," she said in a tremulous voice," it *should* have been a man. She arrived, and we, Miss Atkins, and I agreed she was no good for our church. We hid her in the Almshouses until he arrived, the real vicar that is."

"You held her prisoner?" said Belinda.

Muriel nodded as though it was a new thought. "I suppose we did, really. When he arrived, we had to get rid of her... so we killed her. We bashed her face to hide her identity. That was my idea," she added with a hint of self-importance. "We knew your garden was being repaired, so we buried her there one night. We would have got away with it, that is until we discovered that evil woman claiming to be Madam Malefic, whoever she really is, knew what we had done. She held that power over us, and when the real Madam Malefic bought the cottage, she forced us to kill her as well, so she could pretend to be the new owner. Otherwise, she would tell the police we had murdered Lamb. We had no choice, so we killed her, stabbed her with a carving knife."

"What happened to her body," said Belinda as she tried to take in all this startling information.

Muriel shook her head. "Don't know. We were told she was cremated. That beast, the Captain, took her away, and we were told to keep quiet about her death, or the police would be informed we had committed two murders. To us, it was really only one because the woman vicar should never have been ordained, so she doesn't count," she concluded self-righteously.

Hazel, who had been listening in awe, said, "The knife in the paper bag? Was that the murder weapon that killed Madam Malefic?"

Muriel glanced at her. "Yes. Miss Atkins had lost it, and the Madam was furious with her and wanted it to be retrieved and got rid of. She wanted no evidence at all to be found connecting her with the murder."

"And that's why, after it was found at the theatre that day, she took her to London and drowned her?" said Belinda.

Muriel gave a soft moan and began to weep into her handkerchief.

Chapter Seventeen

In the next few weeks police forensic analysts collected evidence of criminal offenses in the Almshouses. Muriel and Miss Atkins had cleaned up after the murders, but investigators were able to detect traces of blood at the crime scene. Muriel was taken into police custody and charged. She was held under guard in hospital while recovering from intense mental distress and was on suicide watch.

Dental records supplied from Durham confirmed the body in the garden was that of the Reverend Lamb. The nationwide search for Madam Perrot continued with various sightings from Norwich to Liverpool, from Bournemouth to Aberdeen, but all proved to be false.

Quentin had written to say he was staying on in Germany and not returning to Milford until he was required to give evidence to the police. He had placed his cottage in the hands of a real estate manager for sale.

Hazel had returned to her apartment in Lansdown Crescent as the renovations were complete. When she did come by Milford, it was most often to visit Charles, with whom she had formed an odd relationship and was continually supplying him with exotic meals as a precursor to any potential bonding that may eventuate.

So Belinda was, for the first time in many months, alone in the cottage. The Summer had set in and was surprisingly warm, so she slept with the window open to catch the cool night air.

It was on such a night she was woken by a peculiar sound. It took her some time to realise what it was. It drew closer and then faded away. The wild sound of horse and carriage wheels turning, horses hooves striking solid earth.

Madam Perrot had returned!

Flinging on joggers, a top, and running shoes, Belinda sprinted into the night and down the path to Kryme Cottage. The sky was clear, and a bright luminous moon lit the way.

On her approach, the sounds of boisterous activity filled her ears, and she was startled to see the interior of the building brightly it. Nearby, the horses in the carriage were wild-eyed, swishing their tails and tossing their heads. The door had been smashed open, while intense light spilled into the garden.

Cautiously Belinda made her way inside to be greeted with the sight of Madam Perrot, a sinister figure, set in blinding light emanating from numerous work lights. The woman was screaming violent curses and swung a massive sledgehammer to smash against the ancient walls. The stone began to crumble at each impact. Again and again, the woman dealt blow upon blow, each time shouting obscenities mixed with garbled cries, "Five Shillings!" "White Lace!" White Lace!" Belinda stood transfixed as the madwoman continued her rampage, the sound of the blows reverberating into the night.

Unexpectedly she felt two arms around her, crushing her arms to her side, holding her in a firm grip, which lifted her off her feet. Struggling, she saw her captive was the Captain, who leered close to her face. Just as suddenly, she heard a loud thwack, and the Captain released his hold, to collapse back onto the floor, blood flowing from his head.

Standing over him was Darcy's slim figure, holding a large blood covered stone from the wreckage created by Madam. He looked at Belinda with a smile in his eyes and heartily kicked the Captain's inert body.

Madam, distracted by this activity, recognised there was an intruder within her domain. With superhuman strength, she swung the heavy hammer above her head to charge at Belinda.

Terrified, Belinda stumbled over broken stones and rushed for cover, with the furious woman in pursuit, who screamed at her, "You'll not stop me! I know it's here, the white lace, my white lace. They said I stole it. Imprisoned me! But I made fools of them. My niece Jane knew I was innocent. White lace valued at one pound. I deny stealing the lace! The salesclerk gave it to me by mistake. Charged with grand theft, the death sentence! But it's *here*. The white lace. *It's here.* I'll find it! And you'll not stop me!"

Backing away and looking for some way to escape, Belinda reached the wooden staircase and, leaping on to it, scrambled up as far as she could. The decaying wooden structure swayed and screeched from this onslaught.

With a curse, Madam came running forward and swung the hammer to smash against the wooden frame, causing it to partially break free from its attachment to the wall. At the same time, the lower steps fell away, leaving Belinda hanging from what remained, perilously high above the floor.

Madam, an ugly smirk on her lips, eyes blazing with insanity, gave a crazy laugh, and again swung the massive sledgehammer high and brought it down on the wall adjacent to where Belinda was clinging.

The blow sent a deep shudder through the ancient stones, and with a loud rumble, they splintered, disintegrated, and in an explosion of dust and crumbling stone, the wall partly collapsed, burying Madam under the weight of centuries.

Chapter Eighteen

"I thought she was about to release the flying monkeys," said Belinda as she recalled that terrible night. "And I have Darcy to thank for saving me from the Captain, and getting me down safely from the staircase before it and the wall collapsed."

The summer days were fading, and a tantalising impression of Autumn permeated the air. Belinda, Hazel, and Charles gathered at the ruins of Kryme Cottage. Some of the remaining walls were in perilous condition and were roped off for safety. The roof had collapsed, so they stood in the open on the stone floor.

"It seems Madam Perrot had spent time in shelters over the years and was well known to authorities," said Belinda on her return to Milford after attending the trials in London. "She has been found criminally insane and put away in a high security psychiatric hospital. Muriel and the Captain have both been jailed. Muriel for the murder of the reverend Lamb and Madam Malefic, the Captain with aiding and abetting the murder of Miss Atkins."

"And what of Darcy?" asked Hazel.

"He has a reduced sentence, mainly because he had saved me on that terrible night, and he is to be given assistance on his release to help him in the future."

"And what of the poor Madam Malefic? What happened to her body?"

Belinda looked miserable. "You won't believe this. Madam Perrot did have her cremated."

"How," said Charles, "you have to have two doctors approve a death certificate to permit a cremation?"

"Oh, she didn't believe in niceties such as that. She knew people, people who would do anything for money.

"What happened to her ashes?" said Hazel.

"This is the weirdest thing ever. She had them made into a vinyl record. The one she played the night of the seance."

"Ugh!" cried Hazel.

"Can you do that?" said Charles.

"Apparently. Some companies blend the ashes into a recording, usually of the departed's voice."

"I think that's sick," said Hazel wrinkling her lips in disgust.

"Well, it is, and that's what Madam Perrot was. All because she became obsessed with a few feet of white lace, which she believed was hidden by Jane Austen's aunt in Kryme Cottage."

They turned as the sound of a motor drew near, and a large earth-moving machine drove up and onto the floor. Charles spoke to the driver and pointed out a section of the stones. The driver manoeuvred the bucket, and iron teeth sank into the worn limestone blocks and began to break them away from each other.

"I couldn't understand how Madam Perrot

could smash the solid walls so easily," said Belinda.

"Limestone can be affected when rainwater reacts with it, causing it to dissolve," said Charles, "so, over centuries of exposure to the elements, it was possible for her to break off large chunks."

Almost delicately, the bucket scooped up a large slab and removed it, revealing the long-hidden earth beneath. Lifting his arm as an instruction to the driver, who switched off the motor, Charles moved swiftly to the opening and sank to his knees. Belinda and Hazel stood close by wondering what he expected to find.

Pulling on heavy-duty gloves, Charles reached down and took hold of what appeared to be a stone box, about thirty inches by twenty. He called to the driver for assistance, and together they struggled to free the box. Lifting it to the surface, they rested it on the broken floor.

"What is it?" said Belinda as she watched in wonder at the designs etched on the sandstone top.

"It's an ossuary box," said Charles with a note of triumph in his voice. "I suspected it, and now I'm proven right."

"What is it for?"

"An ossuary's a chest, the final resting place of human remains. A body was first buried in a transitory grave, then after several years, the skeletal remains were removed and placed in here."

"But why here?" said Hazel.

"Because I believed that Kryme Cottage was once a small church. Probably late Anglo Saxon, back around the eleventh century. I'd done some research before coming here, and the records make mention of a small chapel or church somewhere in this area. After the Reformation, it closed and eventually got lost as a church and became a private residence. Changes were made over the years, including the Georgian facade that some misguided owner inflicted on the building. It was the windows that convinced me the cottage had a religious past, and of its age."

"Yes," said Belinda, "I noticed them. They're very narrow..."

"With sides splayed out to show the massive depth of the limestone walls. That allowed for more light," confirmed Charles. "Also, the shape. The whole of the building was the nave, and the half circle at the far end was the chancel, where the altar would have been. Just a fundamental structure, before aisles and vestries were added. I was convinced there was a tomb, or an ossuary box buried here, given the age of the building, and the uneven stone floor, which indicated that at some time, it had been disturbed, possibly for a burial.

"But who would it be, the dead person I mean," said Belinda.

"That's anyone's guess, but probably a priest or a monk from that time."

"So that's what your interest was? An old church?"

Charles nodded. Then he turned to the driver. "Help me free the lid."

With the aid of a chisel as a lever, they freed the top cover and gently removed it.
There, in the box, facing the world after centuries, the gathered bones of one long departed soul.

Chapter Nineteen

Belinda stood at her cottage's front door enjoying the light breeze, and looked out over her famous garden. It had been a good summer with garden enthusiasts from all over the world paying homage to Capability Brown. Here and there, a leaf showed a tiny preview of the coming seasonal change and evidence of time passing. With it would bring the end to busloads of tourists, and Milford would settle down comfortably for the winter slumber.

After the excitement of the past months, her mind was filled with memories of her time at the cottage, and all that had transpired since that day years ago, when a buff coloured envelope had dropped into her letterbox, in the tiny apartment she shared with another Australian girl in South Kensington. It led to her friendship with Hazel Whitby and their adventures as amateur sleuths: her engagement to wealthy businessman Sir Mark Salinger, and the subsequent breakup of their relationship: the murder of her old boyfriend from Melbourne and the search for a missing national heirloom: crazed fanatics following a leader who claimed to be the rightful king of England. All that, and much more, stemming from an innocent-looking message.

Addressed in thin spidery handwriting, the letter was brief and to the point.
"Dear Belinda, I would appreciate it if you would

*come down to the cottage this weekend. I have some-
thing of interest for you.*
Yours, Jane Lawrence."

Earlier, when freshly arrived from Australia as an eager nineteen-year-old, she'd tracked down her father's aunt. 'What do you want?' the old lady had said suspiciously as she peered around the weather-beaten door. The aunt eyed her up and down, then nodded abruptly and stepped back to allow her to enter the house. The tall figure, stooped and the hem of her long skirt trailing on the floor, her aunt led the way into a long narrow room that ran the length of the back of the house. The visit wasn't a great success, but she had coaxed the old lady into a grudging familiarity, but those years later she was amazed to discover she was to inherit the cottage and garden.

In answer to her great aunt's written re-quest, she'd taken the train to Bath, and her taxi drove until it came to crossroads where four cot-tages stood one on each corner. It halted outside the sizeable grey stone two-storey cottage. Her reflec-tion sped in erratic liquid manoeuvres across the shrouded windows' uneven glass as she rapped her arrival on the great doorknocker.
Something dark moved on the terrace balustrade, and she'd turned in fright to face it.

A grey rat scuttled for cover.

Before she realised it, she was standing in the entrance hall. The gloom stretched before her, menacing and enigmatic.

She recalled from her previous visit the long sitting room. Crossing to a door leading into the back hall and the staircase, a strong odour increased as she pulled the door towards her. There was the tiny sound of scattering feet.

'Rats!'

Moving tentatively across the dark hall, her foot caught on something solid. She plummeted onto the grimy floor and lay dazed for a moment.

As her eyes had grown accustomed to the faint light from the other room, there came the realisation that only inches away, her aunt Jane's deathly glazed eyes stared accusingly at her.

Belinda shook her head to clear that fateful day's memory and hugged herself as her thoughts returned to the present, and the sunshine that warmed her now.

Hazel was spending more and more time with Charles to the consternation and scorn of the parishioners at Abbey Combe.

Mr and Mrs Lawrence were pestering their daughter to return to Melbourne.

Quentin had emailed her to say he had accepted a commission for a photo essay on Somerset and hoped to see her when he was in England. He had admitted to secretly taking a photo of her on the day of the wedding, and she smiled at the thought.

A slight squeak and a soft caress on her ankle made her look down.

A tiny tabby kitten purred loudly as it

brushed against her in a manner suggestive of ownership.

Belinda stared at it. The creature lifted its head to gaze at her.

The breeze dropped, and the garden was still.

Time was still.

Belinda knew if she was to pick up this creature, embrace it, love it, life was taking her in a new direction.

There was a long moment.

The kitten purred.

Belinda bent down...

Inside the cottage, the telephone rang...

RECIPE:

Chestnut, Bacon & Parsnip Soup

A smooth and creamy winter soup, topped with crispy bacon pieces - serve with crusty bread.

Ingredients

4 chopped rashers smoked streaky bacon

drizzle of olive or rapeseed oil

1 chopped onion

1 crushed garlic clove

6 peeled and chopped parsnips

1 chicken stock cube

400ml milk

leaves from 4 thyme sprigs

200g cooked, chopped chestnuts

To Make:

Fry the rashers of bacon in the oil until crisp. Scoop out half the bacon and set aside. Add the onion and garlic to the pan, stirring until tender, then add the parsnips. Cook for another 5 mins, then crumble in the chicken stock cube. Add the milk, 600ml water, the thyme and chestnuts. Cover and simmer for 30 mins until the parsnip is tender. Blend, then season to taste. Ladle into bowls and top with the reserved bacon.

COCKTAILS:

The Walking Dead
30ml Dry Island Gin
25ml lemon juice
20ml Maidenii La Tonique or Lillet Blanc
10ml sugar syrup
3ml absinthe
Lemon twist, to garnish

Chill a coupette glass. Combine all ingredients
in a cocktail shaker with ice, shake and fine
strain into your glass.

Flaming Fanny
Made with Orange juice, Vodka, Cream Soda.
Ingredients to use:
8oz Orange juice
4oz Vodka
5oz Cream Soda

Directions:
mix together and serve with ice

BRIAN KAVANAGH

CV: https://filmmaker2.webs.com

IMDB: https://www.imdb.com/name/nm0442538/

Books Promo Video: https://vimeo.com/331189458

BLOG: https://thecuttingroomfloor12.blogspot.com